W9-CYD-467

THE WESSEX
PAPERS

DATE DUE			
OCT 1 1 2008			
GAYLORD 234			PRINTED IN U. S. A.

An Imprint of HarperCollins*Publishers*

For information address
HarperCollins Children's Books, a division of
HarperCollins Publishers, 1350 Avenue of the Americas, New York,
NY 10019.

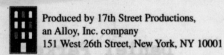 Produced by 17th Street Productions,
an Alloy, Inc. company
151 West 26th Street, New York, NY 10001

Library of Congress Catalog Card Number: 2001118923
ISBN 0-06-440806-X

First Avon edition, 2002

Visit us on the World Wide Web!
www.harperteen.com

Prologue: Sunday Winthrop's Speech to the Graduating Class (as typed)

What's up, Wessex!!!

(Pause for applause.)

Hello, fellow Wessexonians! Hello, parents! Hello, teachers! Hello, seniors!

(Allow fifteen seconds for hooting to die down.)

Well. How do I even begin? Clearly, this graduation isn't like most. I mean, who would have thought that they would pick me to give the commencement address? I've spent four years cleverly shirking any serious responsibility.

(Pause for appreciative laughter.)

But as we all know, this year was different than any other. It was a year marked by wonderful triumph, and marred by what could have been terrible tragedy. It was a year of sordid crimes and bizarre hijinks. And before I begin, let me just say a few things: It's up to us to ensure that the actions of a depraved few don't tarnish the good name of the Wessex Academy. *(Clear throat. Put on a serious face.)* It's up to us to keep the true spirit of Wessex alive as we go forth into the future. A spirit forged by an unparalleled reputation and over 200 years of excellence . . .

(Pause again for applause.)

And I . . . ever . . . pression . . . some . . .

(Tap microphone.) I think . . . ight be a prob . . . *(Tap microphone*

again, mouthing words silently.) . . . oose connection? *(Smile.)* Oh, well . . . uch more to say . . .

(Shrug. Wait for the crowd to start cheering again. Take a bow. Exit.)

Note to self: Shred speech when done.

Part I:
The Waldorf vs. The Marriott
(Nine months earlier)

Sunday Winthrop's contribution to the Wessex Academy's "time capsule": a sealed tube full of anonymous personal essays which is buried at the beginning of every senior year, then unearthed twenty-five years later as an ongoing study of sociological trends at boarding schools. Students are encouraged to "write whatever they feel."

"Membership has its privileges." —American Express

That's going to be my senior quote. I figure if I tell you children of the future my senior quote, then you'll be able to figure out who wrote this little essay. (And if my daughter's among you, hi, honey!) That way I won't be anonymous. After all, what's the point of doing something if you can't take credit for it?

Also, at this particular moment in history, planning a senior quote is a very big deal at Wessex. You start thinking about it as a freshman. As far as I know, nobody has ever used a line from a credit card commercial before. Maybe things will be different twenty-five years from now. Maybe everybody will use credit card commercials. But now it's taboo—too tacky, too gauche. And such a pronouncement even more deep and meaningful coming from me, because I'm one of the lucky few at Wessex who actually *has* a credit card. A platinum card, no less. Everybody in my little circle has a platinum card. Two summers ago, our parents all gathered together and decided to make them a sixteenth birthday present.

That's how most important decisions in our lives are made: Our parents gather together in sumptuous living rooms and drink vodka and tonics, then decide what's best for us.

"Should we give them platinum cards?"

"Oh, yes! Lovely idea. On their sixteenth birthdays."

"Good! It's settled, then. Cheers."

(Here, the clink of V&Ts replaces the sound of a gavel.)

I don't think my friends would ever flaunt their credit cards, though—at least not in the pages of the hallowed *Wessex Encomium*. No, credit cards are to be kept secret and hidden away, used only for a clandestine ski trip or a long weekend in New York City.

That's the beauty of the quote. Somehow, the yearbooks always end up filled with the same garbage year after year: Shakespeare and Kurt Vonnegut and the Beatles and . . . whatever. Either that or secret little messages: "JKC, Confession is good for the soul." Translation: "Dude, I can't believe we got stoned in the chapel!" (Very clever, boys.) It's like there's an unwritten rule: you have to conform to a certain way of being deep or funny, even though your yearbook page is touted as this pure statement of your individuality. It doesn't make any sense. It's kind of hypocritical, isn't it? At least, that's how it's always seemed to me.

So I'm going the route of the corporate catchphrase. A celebration of the American Dream. Why not? Big business has made my family loads of money. Those four words suit me a lot better than any line from *The Tempest* or some song off *Revolver*. They're honest. They're true. Teen angst? Forget about it. I'm part of a select group, the children of the most powerful alums—the elite. "ABs," we're called. "Alumni Brats." We rule the school. Everybody knows it. There's no point in trying to act polite or pretending we're just like everyone else. Membership *does* have its privileges.

I recently read an article in *The New York Times* that said boarding school had changed, that the children of alumni (I think the PC term is *legacies*) no longer had any power. "The snobby, elitist days of *The Catcher in the Rye* are over," it said. What a load of crap! I mean, I can't really remember what happens in *The Catcher in the Rye*, but I know that it reminded me a lot of Wessex. So whoever wrote that *Times* article must have skipped Wessex in their research.

For example, here are some of the rumors about us ABs: We don't have to take the SATs because we're guaranteed college admission (false, although I seriously doubt we'll have any trouble getting in wherever our parents went); we're invited to faculty parties all the time (true, unfortunately); we're Freemasons (what the hell *is* a Freemason, anyway?); we're on a special council with the power to expel other students. . . .

See what I'm getting at?

I think the real problem, though, is that nothing ever touches us. Most people pick a senior quote that reflects a defining moment in their lives. But our lives are totally free of defining moments. That's what I'm really trying to say: There will be no bumps, no highs, no lows, no challenges . . . just a smooth sail. From this moment, until the day you dig up this paper—and even beyond—

we will winter in Aspen and summer in the Hamptons.

And if that sounds great to those of you in the future who aren't ABs, I recommend that you read *No Exit* by Jean-Paul Sartre. It's a play about these three rich jerks who are trapped together in this really nice room. Then they realize that they're in hell. In fact, the big line from the play is: "Hell is other people." That pretty much sums it up for the AB crowd. If you do the same old things enough times with the same old crew . . .

Okay. That sounds pathetic. That *is* pathetic. Here I am, ranting about existential literature and complaining about being trapped in hell, when the fact of the matter is that I'm spoiled rotten . . . but still.

I mean, for one thing, I actually *am* going to be trapped in a really nice room with two rich people. That's right. This year, *senior* year—supposedly the best year of our boarding school lives—Allison Scott, Mackenzie Wilde, and I will all be sharing a suite in our parents' old dorm. The famous "Reed Hall triple." Dad happened to live there with Allison's dad and Mackenzie's dad thirty years ago, so he thought it would be "neato" (his word, not mine) if we followed in their footsteps. Mr. Scott and Mr. Wilde clinked on it. That made it official. Court adjourned. Appeal denied.

Mackenzie, I don't mind. Mackenzie, I'm psyched for. She actually *is* somebody I'd want to have for a roommate. She's like a little sister. No, she's more like Frenchy from *Grease* (I love that movie, and I pray that it's still being watched when you read this—because it's a classic). Mackenzie's got the perpetual bubble gum and the big wide eyes, and she is completely unpolluted by cynicism. Completely unjaded. She still writes notes to herself on her jeans. And she believes in astrology. She *really* believes. She also thinks she's the reincarnation of Janis Joplin. She doesn't grind her teeth, either. Allison grinds her teeth all the time. . . .

Okay, I don't want to sound like a whiner. I can handle the teeth-grinding. I'm sure I have some annoying tics, myself. I can even handle Allison's Seven-Part Life Plan. (I found it in her room last year. Part Five is having an affair with her dog breeder.) No, the one thing that still really bothers me about Allison is how she told me that I wasn't good enough to be her friend.

We were ten years old. We were playing at Allison's house in East Hampton, trying on her mother's jewelry (the way we always did when our parents were downstairs having cocktails) and I put on this long string of pearls and marched around the room pretending to be Allison's mother, with my eyebrows up and my chin out (Mackenzie was there, too; she was cracking up, because it *was* funny) . . . and out of the blue, Allison just glared at me and said that I had no business making fun of her mother. Nor, apparently, did I have any business being her friend, because—drum roll, please—I wasn't "good enough." Then she stalked out of the room.

But maybe I've made too big a deal out of it. Sure, I've thought about it almost every day for the last seven years. But that's probably due to a chemical imbalance or something—like I'm not getting enough oat bran, so my brain is stuck on rewind. And sure, it's also the kind of thing that would make a shrink sit up and say, "Aha! No wonder you're so screwed up and unhappy!" But I don't see a shrink. My family doesn't believe in shrinks. How could we? We live in Greenwich. Mom can trace her ancestry back to the Mayflower. Dad is in the Goose Hunting Club. If anyone can find me a Wessex alum who hunts geese *and* sees a shrink, I'll surrender my trust fund. And I really hope that things will change in twenty-five years. I really do. Because I know that Mom and Dad have problems—who doesn't?—but they just use V&Ts and witty banter to hide them, like strategic smudges of cover-up over big, fat zits. . . .

Wait, what was I talking about?

Oh, right—about how I feel trapped in hell. But try to see it my way. It makes no difference if I'm "good enough" to be Allison's friend. It never has. I have no choice but to be Allison's friend. Our parents clinked a V&T on *that* one before we were even born.

So. Maybe I ought to reconsider "Membership has its privileges." Maybe I should go with "Hell is other people."

Seeing a shrink might not be a bad idea, either.

1

I should be wearing a dominatrix outfit. With stiletto heels. And a clown nose.

These were Sunday Winthrop's first thoughts as Mom and Dad hustled her out of the afternoon sunshine and into the dark foyer of Headmaster Olsen's mansion.

Well actually that wasn't quite true. These were her *second* thoughts. Her first thought was that somebody should finally suggest to Headmaster Olsen that he give up on the comb-over. Gently, of course. The poor guy. She tried to smile as she shook his hand. Oh, the humanity. She'd watched him fight a desperate battle with male pattern baldness for—what, now? Fifteen years?

"How are you, Sunday?"

"Fine, thanks, Mr. Olsen. And you?"

"Oh, same as always. Heh, heh, heh."

He wasn't lying. Sunday had been barely two years old when Dad brought her here for the first time—for his fifteenth reunion. (Yikes. That meant Dad's *thirtieth* reunion was this fall. Which meant another alumni bash from hell. Was it too late to apply for an exchange program in Siberia?) In the intervening years, Dad had matured into a happy-go-lucky, graying, Richard Gere–type. Mom had discovered hobbies, like watercolor painting. Sunday herself had become a young woman, complete with cleavage. But Olsen hadn't changed a bit, except for the loss of a few more hairs. He still had that ruddy face. That bow tie. Those beige slacks. Not pants. *Slacks.* That wide-wale corduroy jacket . . .

But back to the stilettos and clown nose.

The problem was this: The moment Sunday walked in the door, she saw that Allison was wearing the exact same Lily Pulitzer dress as she was. Now normally Sunday would laugh at this kind of snafu. ("Oh, look," somebody was sure to say. "How cute. Sunday and Allison are wearing the same outfit. Just like when they were kids!") But Allison had called Sunday the night before, for the express purpose of avoiding such a coincidence:

Allison:	"So what are you going to wear at Olsen's tomorrow?"
Sunday:	"Not sure yet. I was thinking about that Lily Pulitzer dress."
Allison:	"The one I have?"
Sunday:	"Yeah? Why? Are you going to wear it?"
Allison:	"Oh, no. Too conservative."
Sunday:	"You think so?"
Allison:	"Definitely. I want to make a splash. It *is* the first day of senior year."

Yet there Allison was, in Olsen's living room—standing solo among the plates of hors d'oeuvres and the shelves full of leather-bound books . . . in the Lily Pulitzer. Right by the rolltop desk. On the first day of senior year. Classic. Sunday shook her head. *Splash, my ass.* She knew exactly what Allison had been thinking. Oh, yes. She knew the Allison strategy from a lifetime of experience. Allison had been planning on wearing the Lily Pulitzer from the get-go. So she'd made a preemptive strike. She wanted Sunday to *doubt* the Lily Pulitzer. To make Sunday think that it *was* a little too conservative. To play on Sunday's fashion insecurities. And when Sunday went with the splash herself, Allison would counterstrike with the Lily. . . .

Whatever. It was funny. It was ridiculous, actually.

Sunday knew she shouldn't get angry, because getting angry was something Allison would do. She should appreciate the silliness of it all. Hey, at least she didn't look like Nicole Kidman. At least she had her own thing going: skinny frame, long dark hair, no immediate celebrity resemblances. Allison's resemblance to Nicole Kidman was terrifying, right down to that little button nose. She was a full-fledged clone. (Oddly enough, though, Allison spoke like Madonna, post-elocution lessons—thanks to years of etiquette camp. Her accent fell somewhere between JFK and the Queen of England.)

"Aren't you going to go say hi to Allison, honey?" Dad asked.

No, thanks.

"She's standing all by herself," Mom said.

Maybe she forgot to wear deodorant.

"Oh, look!" Headmaster Olsen exclaimed. "You two have the same dress. How cute!"

Sunday smiled. "It is cute, isn't it?" she said.

Allison pretended not to notice them. This was a fairly difficult feat, considering that she was less than fifteen feet away—and alone. But she doggedly chewed on a stuffed mushroom and stared at a spot on the wall just above Olsen's antique globe. The "lost-in-thought" look, Sunday supposed. God help them all. Where was Mackenzie, anyway?

"The party's out back," Olsen said. "Come, come. Let's have a drink, shall we?"

"Is Mackenzie out there?" Sunday asked.

"No, I'm afraid the Wildes aren't here yet," Olsen said. He whisked Mom and Dad into the living room, heading for the back door. "Oh, that reminds me. Thanks for your timely submission for the time capsule! Mackenzie hasn't sent hers in yet. . . ."

"Hi, Allison!" Mom called.

Sunday's smile became strained.

"Oh, hi, Mr. and Mrs. Winthrop!" Allison shook her head and smiled as they hurried past her. "I didn't see you."

Dad jerked his head toward Sunday before disappearing around the corner. "Look who's here," he cried jovially. "Roomie number two!"

Thanks, Dad. Thanks for reminding me.

Allison turned to her. Her own fake smile faltered—just for an instant. Then she started grinding her teeth.

"Hey, what do you know?" Sunday said. "We wore the same dress. Maybe Mackenzie will, too. Then we'll be like sisters. Triplets."

"Right," Allison said. She seemed confused.

Sunday swallowed. Now came the hard part.

Did they do the "hello hug," or didn't they?

14

There was really no reason to do the hello hug. Sunday had seen Allison only a week ago, out in East Hampton. The hello hug was usually reserved for seeing a dear friend after a long time. A month or more. On the other hand, they *had* done the hello hug every year so far at Olsen's annual AB Welcome Party. It was a ritual. It was *formal*. And that was the kicker: Allison was big on formalities. So she'd probably go for it.

Then again . . . maybe she wouldn't. Maybe she could sense Sunday's hesitation. Or maybe the embarrassment over the dress would preempt the hello hug.

All right, worst case scenario: Sunday would go for the hello hug, and Allison would hesitate, and then Sunday would hesitate, too—and they'd end up in some kind of awkward little *non-hug* which they would both try to laugh off, making the whole thing that much more excruciating. . . .

Why is my life so very, very lame?

Sunday smiled at Allison. Allison smiled back. The seconds ticked by.

"You look pretty, Sun," Allison said.

"You too, Al," Sunday replied.

"Thanks." Allison nodded toward the tray table of stuffed mushrooms. "You should try those. They're really good."

And that settled it. Sigh of relief. Allison had deftly guided them into the midst of a conversation, bypassing opening pleasantries, so there was no longer any need for the hello hug. Nor, apparently, was there any need to talk further about the dress. *Well done, Al,* Sunday silently congratulated her. *Well done.*

"So how come you're not outside with everyone else?" she asked, heading straight for the mushrooms.

"I'm waiting for Hobson," Allison said. "We're supposed to discuss something."

Sunday suppressed a grin. Hobson was Allison's boyfriend. His full name was Mortimer Hobson Crowe III. Allison had been going out with him since sophomore year. He was tall, blond, and blue-eyed. He sort of looked like a cross between the *Dawson's Creek* guy and a young Robert Redford. He had what people used to call "moneyed good looks." Members of his family had been at Wessex for five generations, earning him the longest lineage of any AB.

Ergo: He was Allison's ideal mate. *Was* being the key word.

Last year, however, he came down with a severe case of IFTHS (I'm-From-The-Hood Syndrome). The symptoms were sudden and baffling, as they often are. He'd started wearing a black wool hat. His baggy pants hung low. He flashed signs for nonexistent gangs. His friends became his "dawgs." Everything he said came in a "yo" sandwich; all utterances began and ended with "yo." (Example: "Yo, where my dawgs at, yo?") He even took to writing his own raps, referring to himself as "Sir Mack-A-Lot."

"Yo, you know I rock a party in style.
Sir Mack-A-Lot's here to get buck wild. . . ."

IFTHS was fairly common, of course. Sunday figured it struck about one out of every five white males at some point or another, to some degree. Even at Wessex it had reached the proportions of a minor epidemic. Still, this was the first time it had ever happened to a good friend, an AB—one of their own. And Hobson seemed like the unlikeliest candidate of all. He was from New Canaan, for God's sake. His mother used to dress him in a little sailor's uniform.

Still, the condition did have its upsides. The most beautiful and demented of these was that Allison refused to acknowledge that any change had taken place. Almost overnight, Mortimer Hobson Crowe III had become the latest hip-hop sensation (in his own mind), but Allison pretended not to notice. Having a "homey" for a boyfriend simply wasn't part of her Seven-Part Life Plan. People would rag on him; she would brush them off. As far as Allison was concerned, Hobson had to be perfect, so he *was* perfect. Case closed.

Hobson, to his credit, always took the heat with the same good-natured reply: "Yo, whatever, I'm keepin' it real, yo." *Keepin' it real.* How? By not tucking his shirt in? Everyone laughed behind his back—or to his face—but he didn't seem to care. He actually seemed to have fun with it. He would make Allison mix tapes. She would go out of her way to tell Sunday and Mackenzie how sweet he was. The tapes were filled with songs like "Big Pimpin'" and "I Want a Gangsta Bitch." Sunday wished more than anything that she could videotape their conversations when they were alone. Maybe Hobson called Allison his "Gangsta Bitch." For all Sunday knew, it went both ways. Maybe Allison called him her "Big Pimp."

"This is so typical," Allison muttered under her breath.

"What is?" Sunday asked, reaching for a mushroom.

"He refuses to discuss what we're going to wear to the Harvest Ball."

"But that isn't until October," Sunday said.

Allison frowned at her. "That's exactly what *he*

said. The point is, I wanted to discuss it with him *now*—with his parents present—so Mrs. Crowe will know the specific brand of cummerbund I want him to wear with his tuxedo. I was planning for it to match my dress—"

Hobson suddenly burst through the kitchen door, nearly tripping on the tattered hem of his pants. All his clothes were at least two sizes too big.

He froze when he saw them. His eyes bulged. He gave them both a once-over.

"Damn, yo!" he cried gleefully. "Wassup, dawgs? Those dresses are *ill*." He shook his head and grabbed a handful of mushrooms, stuffing them into his mouth at once. "Y'all look like a Doublemint commercial."

Sunday grinned. Sweet, sweet Hobson. "You hear that, Al?" she asked. "We look like a Doublemint commercial."

Allison didn't answer. She was busy grinding her teeth again.

An hour later, when Mackenzie finally showed up, Sunday had somehow managed to get herself cornered by Headmaster Olsen and Winslow Ellis— "Winnie"—in the backyard.

Being stuck with Olsen wouldn't have been *so* bad. True, he was going on and on about the varsity basketball team, a subject in which Sunday had about as much interest as, say, any other sport—but there was something cute about his excitement. It was so *genuine*. Sunday's father had played basketball for Wessex, so Olsen naturally assumed that Sunday would be thrilled about the new talent coming in this year, some whiz from Washington, D.C. . . . That was the defining feature of Olsen's personality: He honestly believed that ABs were younger versions of their parents. Chips off the old block, as it were.

Winnie, on the other hand . . . *Blecch.* Talk about the antithesis of genuine. Everything about him was fake. Well, except for his suit: It was made of summer wool. But that was it. Even his *body* was fake. The guy had clearly undergone some major reconstructive surgery over the summer. The dark caterpillar on his forehead had been severed and trimmed, leaving him two perfect eyebrows. His nose was smaller, too. And his chin looked more pointy. Sadly, though, the surgeons couldn't do anything about his blubbery hips. Or the rest of his body hair. (Actually, it was closer to fur.) Maybe Winnie would have to wait until he was older for the electrolysis and liposuction. Or maybe Olsen wanted him to stay fat; Winnie was the basketball team's center, and Olsen was saying something about a big presence in the middle. . . .

"That's what it's going to take to beat Carnegie Mansion in the exhibition game," Winnie confirmed. "Defense. Strong defense."

Olsen nodded. "That's true. But the best defense, as we well know, is a good *offense*."

The two of them chuckled.

"So is this new kid . . ." Winnie snapped his fingers.

"Fred Wright."

"Yes. Is this Fred Wright *really* that good?"

Olsen nodded. "He can carry an entire game if called upon."

Who on earth cares? Sunday's smile grew pained. Olsen's cuteness was rapidly wearing thin. She could feel herself starting to get panicky. *This is my future*, she realized. Yes, this was as good as it was going to get, as far as senior year went: getting stuck with Olsen and Winnie at lame AB functions and being forced to pretend to listen to them. *My God.* The boredom was lethal. Wasn't there a Greek myth about that? Yeah, there was . . . it was about a king who was bored to death by a dull story. What was his name? Her retention was so lousy when it came to history. . . .

Thankfully, at that moment Mackenzie swooped in and yanked Sunday out of the conversation.

"Something's going on between Al and Hobson,"

Mackenzie whispered urgently, dragging Sunday across the manicured lawn toward the back door of the mansion. "Something big. I heard them fighting. I *knew* it. I checked all of our star charts this morning—you know, first day of senior year and all—and guess what the horoscope said? Leos are supposed to watch out for 'confrontation in their love lives.'" She made little quotation marks in the air with her fingers.

Sunday smiled. Ah, Mackenzie. Sunday never had to worry about a worst case hello-hug scenario with Mackenzie. The girl's social skills were non-existent. It was one of the greatest things about her: She was too wrapped up in the world of star charts and horoscopes and her friends' futures to be awkward or even polite. Especially when it came to good gossip. Anything going on between Hobson and Allison was bound to be entertaining. As long as Mom and Dad didn't see them making an escape . . .

"Where are you going, honey?" Dad called.

But of course, they would.

Sunday glanced over her shoulder. "To get some more stuffed mushrooms," she answered.

Dad grinned crookedly. He seemed to be swaying a bit. He was clutching an empty plastic cup in one hand. "Did you hear the news?"

"About the basketball team?" Sunday asked.

He laughed. "No, no—about your chair. They found the chair that I had when I was a student here!"

Sunday hesitated, still smiling. She had no idea how she was supposed to respond to that statement. *The chair?*

"Get this," he added. "You know how they knew it was mine? I'd carved my initials in the seat. Back then, that would have gotten me expelled. But now it's a piece of nostalgia. Like the time capsule! Ha! Anyway, it was in room two-oh-three in Ellis Hall, and they took it out and gave it to you. . . ."

Best just to leave. Dad was clearly floundering in the sea of Olsen's cocktails. He was still talking, in fact, as Sunday pushed Mackenzie through the door into the kitchen.

" . . . real piece of history . . ."

"How many V&Ts has he had?" Mackenzie asked, giggling.

"I'd say three," Sunday muttered. "So where are they?"

"Upstairs."

Sunday followed her, snaking her way through Olsen's first floor—through all the little corridors, past all the Colonial knickknacks and paintings of various Wessex buildings. They were all done by artists who had attended the school, no doubt. The wooden floorboards creaked under their feet. For about the hundredth time, Sunday realized how absolutely perfect this house was for Olsen. It was a portrait of him. It was stodgy, cute, and it never changed.

"Hey, speaking of Ellis Hall, where's Noah?" Mackenzie whispered. "He always makes me laugh at these parties."

Sunday grinned. "Noah Percy makes you laugh because he's a total freak."

"Oh, come on," Mackenzie said. "You *love* Noah."

That was true, actually. Sunday did love Noah—precisely because he *was* a total freak. Also, he had a major crush on her. Being around him was always good for a boost in the old self-esteem department.

"But can you believe that Noah *chose* to live in Ellis?" Mackenzie whispered. "I mean, Mr. Burwell lives there. That guy was *definitely* a serial killer in his past life."

Sunday shrugged. "Noah's always been a glutton for punishment."

Mackenzie paused at the bottom of the stairwell. She glanced over her shoulder, a serious expression on her face. "Shh," she whispered.

"Gotcha." Sunday bit her lip to keep from laughing.

Mackenzie started tiptoeing up the stairs.

Sunday followed as quietly as possible. The floorboards were creaking again. Mackenzie paused at the top of the landing and pointed to a door at the end of the hall: Olsen's bedroom. It was open—just a crack. Two muffled voices drifted out into the hall. Sunday strained her ears.

" . . . don't understand it," Allison said with a sniffle.

Sunday's smile vanished. Wow. Allison actually sounded *sad*. This *was* a big deal.

"Yo, Al—why you buggin'?" Hobson asked. "You know we got to end this. A playa's got to be free."

Wait a second, Sunday thought. She stared at Mackenzie. *Is Hobson—*

"But what about the Harvest Ball?" Allison shrieked. "Or forget about the Harvest Ball, what about the Gold and Silver? We already have tickets! And reservations at the Plaza! You can't do this to me—"

"Come on, Al. We can't stay together just to go to some party. That's like . . . like Eric B. & Rakim getting back together just to do a reunion concert. It's kinda wack, yo. You gotta do it for the *looove*. For real. Know what I'm sayin'?"

Sunday's eyes widened.

Mackenzie cupped her hands over her mouth.

Oh, my God. Hobson was dumping Allison.

This was big. This was *huge*. The poor girl! Talk about a major, major crimp in the Seven-Part Life Plan . . .

Mackenzie tugged on Sunday's sleeve, then hurried back downstairs.

Sunday frowned. Where was she going? This was just getting good.

"Come on," Mackenzie mouthed. "We shouldn't be listening to this."

For a moment, Sunday stood there. Why shouldn't they be listening? This was the kind of once-in-a-lifetime gossip that would keep the Wessex rumor mill churning for years. And they were the first ones on the scene. . . .

Then she sighed.

Okay. Mackenzie felt sorry for Allison. Of course she did. Mackenzie was *nice*. And Sunday supposed that she felt sorry for Allison, too. After all, the girl had put all her eggs in the Sir Mack-A-Lot basket, and now that basket had been tossed into the proverbial recycling bin.

Deep down, though, Sunday had to admit to something: Witnessing this breakup mostly made her feel sorry for herself. Yes—it was pitiful but true. Because Allison was having one of those defining, life-changing, senior-quote moments. A time-capsule moment. And that meant a lot. At the very least, Allison had known *some* romance in the recent past. She'd known *some* drama. *Some* love.

Sunday, on the other hand, hadn't had a boyfriend since the tenth grade. She hadn't even kissed anyone . . . not since Boyce Sutton had tried to unbutton her shirt and she'd slapped him in the face—simultaneously ending their relationship and earning herself a reputation as a huge prude among Boyce's friends. That was *her* last bit of drama: She'd been labeled a nun.

Of course, she couldn't care less about what Boyce's friends thought about her. Well, except maybe for Carter Boyce. He was kind of cute. But his last name was the same as Boyce's first name, and that could get a little weird; if they ever got together, it might be like fooling around with Boyce's brother or something.

Actually, that wasn't weird. No. What was weird was that there were only about five guys at Wessex whom she could possibly date without majorly freaking out her friends and family, and two of them—nearly half—were named "Boyce" in one way or another.

But it was best not to think about that. It was too depressing.

First draft of Fred Wright's application essay for a postgraduate year at the Wessex Academy.

In 1,000 words or less, please describe what you consider to be the defining moment of your life so far.

That's easy. The defining moment of my life was my relationship with Diane. And by that, of course, I mean the end of it.

She dumped me in January. Almost nine months ago. There I was, living the ultimate senior-year fantasy: I was with a beautiful girl, a *college* girl, no less—somebody who had sat in a stuffy interview room and actually *impressed* a college admissions person. . . . Yes, Diane was perfect. Or so I thought. The dresses. The Birkenstocks. The blond hair that goes on and on. She looks like she could have been plucked from the original Woodstock and transplanted into the twenty-first century.

But one day she just came up to me and said, "Salvatore called."

At the time, I didn't know which was worse—that her old boyfriend had called her, or that she'd actually gone out with a guy named Salvatore. I mean, come on. That's a dish you order at an Italian restaurant, not a name. "I'll have the Chicken Salvatore, please." His last name is Viverito. Salvatore Viverito. Isn't that a character on *The Sopranos*?

Oh, wait. Am I offending you? I forgot that Salvatore Viverito actually attended your fine institution. He's a Wessex alum. (I'll be addressing *that* later in this essay.) Yes, my fault. I apologize.

Anyway, it didn't make much sense that Diane would want to get back together with him. I mean, the only reason she hung out with me (and the only reason she even *met* me, actually) was because her freshman dorm was filled with all these stuck-up, private-school losers—spoiled swine like Salvatore Viverito—whom she hated because they were all the same. You see, she went to your archrival, another lame-ass boarding school called Carnegie Mansion. . . .

Whatever. It's cool. I'm past being bitter.

We met at a club. The Black Cat. To call the neighborhood "sketchy" would be euphemistic. The block is home to hookers and thieves. But everybody I know hangs out there on Friday nights, because it's the one place in D.C. where you can feel dangerous and still be relatively safe, as long as you're inside the club doors. It's the one place where you can bang your head with hipsters and enjoy nonalcoholic beverages (they stamp all us underage folk)—the one place where you say to yourself: "Something's gonna go down tonight. Something real."

And then it happened. Last September, when a folk punk trio named Willa Catheter was playing, I met Diane at the bar. We both ordered seltzers, and the bartender got them mixed up. (Mine was lemon-lime; hers was unflavored.) We just started talking. I didn't even know she was a freshman at Georgetown. She didn't tell me that until later—until after I told her that I *lived* in Georgetown. As in the neighborhood.

Diane dug that I was a senior in a public high school. I mean, she really dug it. She'd never been to public school, never even been inside one. She grew up in some huge apartment on Park Avenue in New York City. Her building has six different doormen.

She was always asking me what Lincoln High was like: Did I get frisked coming in the doors? Could people actually learn anything in the overcrowded classrooms? Were teachers terrified of the students?

At first I wanted to impress her. Hell, yeah—I got a knife pulled on me once, but I schooled the guy, and now he's doing time in Sing Sing . . . that kind of BS always made her laugh. Actually, Lincoln was pretty mellow. I didn't learn all that much, I guess. But schoolwork was never a huge priority. I mean, it was the same old score: show up, don't fall asleep in class, crank out a semiliterate paper every now and then that plagiarizes from the *Encyclopedia Britannica*. . . .

Whoops. Maybe I shouldn't be telling you all these things. Ah, who cares?

I spent most of the time playing hoops. I was the baddest point guard since Allen Iverson. Last year, my senior year, we won the regional conference finals.

But you already know that.

That's another thing: Before I met Diane, my life was all about basketball. I never read anything outside the classroom except for *Sports Illustrated*. And *Encyclopedia Britannica*, I guess. I wore a backwards red baseball cap, like the Limp Bizkit guy. I had a really short crew cut. Every other word out of my mouth was "Dude!" It sort of makes me laugh to think about it. I never listened to any music recorded before the year 1996. At least not if I could help it.

Then Diane introduced me to a whole other world. She played me "Castles Made of Sand" by Jimi Hendrix. A song that my mom dug. A song I'd heard maybe twice before. And when I first listened to that sweet backwards guitar solo—I mean, really *listened*—and closed my eyes and drank in the raw beauty of those tragic lyrics and that primal, hypnotic drumbeat . . . it was like being swept out to sea on a tidal wave and plunged down into the coral reefs until I thought my lungs would explode. I'm not kidding. It was *that* good.

Also, Diane couldn't believe that I'd never read any books outside of school. She started lending me everything she could get her hands on. The first book ever was called *Psychotic Reactions and Carburetor Dung*. I still have it. It was by a guy named Lester Bangs, a rock critic who lived fast and died young and believed that rock music is the key to salvation. (Diane believes that, too. Or she pretended to believe that, anyway—before Salvatore reappeared.) My vocabulary started improving. Now I actually use words like *euphemistic* in conversation.

And then she dumped me.

"I just feel getting back together with Salvatore is the right thing to do at this stage in my life," she said. "Things were just too complicated in the past, because we weren't at the same school." I think that was what she said. It was either that or, "Mind if I rip out your heart with my fiendish demon claws?" I couldn't really hear her. There was a lot of background noise at the time. We were at the Black Cat again. The band that night was Thick Meat Sandwich.

But what a lame excuse! She and Salvatore aren't at the same school *now*, either. Salvatore doesn't go to Georgetown. At least, I don't think he does. Not that it matters. No, because at that moment, it all became clear. Her relationship with Salvatore had never ended. I was just the halftime entertainment. The boy-toy.

She tried me on, just like she tried on the Birkenstocks and the tie-dyes, and then she decided, "Jeez, this doesn't really fit."

Well, good for her. Unfortunately, this whimsical decision was a little harder on me. My grades took a nosedive. I stopped going to class. I was sharper, better-read, more open-minded than I had ever been, but it didn't do me a damn bit of good. I stopped eating and sleeping. I even stalked her. Not seriously or anything—but once I snuck into her house when she was away and ransacked her room, looking for anything of mine she might still have, and I found this awful, cheesy, semiliterate letter that Salvatore had written her proclaiming his love, so I stole it and turned it into a dartboard.

And that's not even the worst of it.

Nope. That's not even the bummer to end all bummers. See, I'd been planning to go to Georgetown—to join Diane, to play for a killer basketball team, to be close enough to home to throw parties when my mom went out of town . . . but as you well know, I found out in April they wouldn't accept me. Nope. My grades had fallen too far, too fast.

So now the only way I can possibly get in there is if I take what's called a "postgraduate" year at your fine institution. That's what my college adviser recommended. My mom agreed. I understand that the Wessex Academy is located out in the middle of Connecticut, on all these rolling hills. A mere hour and a half from Carnegie Mansion, in fact. What do you know! And according to your brochure, you're supposed to have (among other things) four gyms, a "science center," and a music library with over 10,000 CDs.

I mean, Jesus—is that ironic, or what? Diane started dating me as a symbolic rebellion against your world. And now that we've broken up, as punishment, I'm actually asking to spend the better part of a year with you. At Salvatore's alma mater, no less.

Oh, right—coincidentally, your basketball team needs help. Funny how that works. You're gonna use me. But that's okay. I can use you right back. I *will* use you right back. Because now I know how it's done. I was taught by the master herself. If Diane taught me anything (besides the fact that Jimi Hendrix rules), it's that you gotta use people if you want to get ahead in this world. You gotta look out for Number One.

And that's what I'm going to do.

So this is my plan. I'm going to go to your school. I'm going to take your goddamn basketball team to the very top of your lame-ass conference. And then I'll get into whatever college I want to. Georgetown? Please. Try Stanford. Or Yale. And while I'm kicking butt on and off the court, I'm going to hook up with as many shallow, stupid, phony boarding-school chicks as possible. (Hey—maybe Salvatore has a sister!) And I'm going to dump all of them.

Because nobody's going to take advantage of me anymore. Nobody's going to trick me into anything. Watch out, Wessex. Here comes Fred Wright.

Wait, that's probably more than 1,000 words, isn't it? Oh, well. I guess I needed to get a few things off my chest. Good thing pencils have erasers.

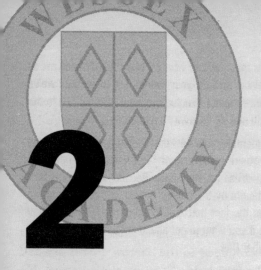

2

Just Fred's luck: His new La-Z-Boy wouldn't fit through the door.

He scowled and wiped the sweat from his forehead. He couldn't believe it. After all that work—after the thirty-minute walk from campus into downtown New Farmington (yes, he was going to be stuck in a place called "New Farmington" for the better part of a year), after finding this kick-ass La-Z-Boy at the only secondhand shop in town, Second Hand News . . . he was stuck.

He'd even wrestled the big, vinyl-clad chair from a cab all the way to the second floor. By himself. Up a spiral staircase, no less. He'd scuffed the walls; he'd groaned and grunted; his back was killing him. But he'd done it. Alone. The rest of his belongings were already inside. The sum total of his life—two duffel bags, a trunk, a suitcase, Salvatore's letter to Diane, and a milk crate full of tapestries (gifts from Diane before the breakup; she'd been good for something)—had been sitting on the floor of his new room for hours now. He'd moved those by himself, too.

All that remained was the La-Z-Boy.

So. *One more try.* Summoning what was left of his strength, he crouched in the narrow dormitory hall and lowered his shoulder against the armrest. He took a deep breath and shoved as hard as he could. But once again, it simply rammed into the door frame.

"Dammit," he whispered.

This was a two-man job. No doubt about it. He'd have to find somebody to lend him a hand, to grab the base and flip the chair around sideways. He stood up and shook his head, glancing down the deserted hall. He should have known he would need help. Everything else about his first day at the prestigious Wessex Academy had pretty much sucked. Why should this be any different?

For starters, his new room was a prison cell. Really. He wasn't being overly dramatic. What was the point of being dramatic when you were alone? He wasn't thinking in metaphor or simile, either.

No. The room wasn't *like* a prison cell. It wasn't "prison-cell-esque." True, he had been sentenced to serve time here for the next nine months, with only intermittent furloughs for holidays. But that was just symbolism.

Room 203 of Ellis Hall *was* a prison cell.

It was about eight feet by eight feet (tops), with one window. Hardly any light made it through the glass, because it was covered by a thick metal grate. The walls were bare white cinderblock. The floor was an uneven puke-green linoleum. The only furniture consisted of a battered wooden desk and a dresser, both of which looked as if they had been dug out of a Sears dumpster sometime during the seventies. Three words were sloppily carved into the top dresser drawer: ME SO HORNY.

Oh, yeah: There was a bed, too. It was completely rusted. Its legs were bolted to the floor. It didn't have sheets or a pillow. All it had was a mattress—the kind of thin, striped, prison mattress that was only wide enough for one skinny person. Fred was skinny, thank God. If he'd been fat, he wouldn't have fit. In the middle of the mattress was a large brown stain, about the size and shape of a manhole cover.

But that wasn't even the worst part. No, the worst part was that the desk chair was missing. Or maybe it had never existed. Maybe the Wessex Academy didn't provide chairs for its students. Maybe he was supposed to stoop all year to do his homework. He had no idea *what* the deal was, because his dorm adviser—some guy named Mr. Burwell—was missing as well. Which was why he schlepped all the way to town to buy this La-Z-Boy in the first place. . . .

Fred glared at it.

Mr. Burwell should be helping him with this. Wasn't that his job? To ease Fred's transition to boarding school life? The lady at the admissions office had promised Fred that Mr. Burwell ("a Wessex Institution," whatever the hell that meant) would be here to greet him upon his arrival. Then again, she'd also promised Fred that Ellis Hall was the best dorm on campus. By way of proof, she'd given him a copy of the Wessex orientation handbook, which featured a photograph of said dorm on the cover. And from the outside, Ellis Hall *did* make a nice picture: It was a cozy white Victorian with black shutters and a porch and a tower for the spiral staircase. For some reason, though, the woman had neglected to mention that the house had been gutted and turned into a cell block. But maybe Fred actually had to read the orientation handbook to find that out. Not that he had any intention of doing so.

"Cool! A La-Z-Boy!"

Fred whirled around.

Okay, *this* . . . this was just perfect. Standing before him at the top of the spiral staircase was a kid straight out of New-England-Boarding-School Central Casting. It was unbelievable. Un-freaking-believable. Diane was right! These kids *were* all the same. Fred had *pictured* this guy—right down to the rumpled, longish brown hair and the tweed blazer and the Polo Oxford and the . . . no, no—could it be? Of course it could. A pair of those L.L. Bean boat shoes. Bluchers. Christ.

Well, luckily, Fred was prepared. He may not have been prepared for the chairless prison cell, but he was prepared for *this*. He knew the score. The Wessex kids were from a world of yachts and mansions and servants—a world where you didn't have to wipe your own butt—and Fred was from the street. (Okay, Fred's street was actually in a wealthy neighborhood, and his mom's townhouse had been cited once in *Architectural Digest*—but he'd gone to public school. *That* was what counted.) So he was going to play it cool. Tough and aloof. Gritty. The Stranger. Yup. That was the new Fred Wright. He'd ask this guy for help and then be done with him.

"This chair is awesome," the guy said. He bent down beside it and ran a hand over the armrest. "How did you clear it with Burwell?"

"I didn't," Fred said defiantly.

The guy glanced up at him. "Uh-oh," he said.

"Why should I have cleared it with Mr. Burwell?" Fred asked.

The guy grinned. "It's just that he's kind of a stickler for the rules about furniture."

Rules about furniture. Fred rolled his eyes. That figured. This place probably had rules about how much water you could use when you took a shower.

"I would have asked him, but he isn't around," Fred said. He pointed through the door at his shabby desk. "Besides, I don't have a chair. I have to sit *somewhere*. So I took a cab into town and bought this La-Z-Boy. I found it at Second Hand News for ten bucks." He knew he sounded overly pleased with himself, but he couldn't help it. He *was* pleased with himself. He could have just sat around here and moped, waiting for Mr. Burwell—or anyone, really—to explain why he didn't have a chair. But the new Fred Wright wasn't a moper.

The kid nodded gravely. "That's funny. I didn't have a chair *my* first year, either. The doctors say it gave me scoliosis. And spinal curvature is permanent, you know. I'll be lucky if I'm able to walk past the age of twenty-five." He smiled again and extended a hand. "But enough of my yakking. My name's Noah. Noah Percy. I live in the single on the first floor. It has its own bathroom."

Fred hesitated, peering at him suspiciously. Then he shook Noah's hand and quickly dropped it. "Fred Wright," he said. "Hey, can I ask you a favor?"

"You need a hand with this thing?" Noah asked.

"Uh . . . yeah." Fred smiled. "If that's cool. . . ."

"No problem," Noah said.

Noah stepped in front of the La-Z-Boy. After giving it a quick study, he abruptly collapsed into it, shifting it into relax mode, with the footrest and headrest fully extended.

"Ahh," he murmured. He stretched and wriggled his feet. "That's the stuff."

"I thought you were gonna give me a hand," Fred said.

"Hey, I just told you I had scoliosis, didn't I? I just gotta take it easy for a sec. One wrong move, and my spine will crack like a toothpick." Noah closed his eyes and sighed. "You know, it's a good thing I caught you before Burwell did. There are a couple of things you should know about him."

"Really," Fred said.

"Yup. For starters, you shouldn't make any fat

jokes around him. Mr. Burwell is grotesquely fat. Most math teachers are."

"Anything else?"

Noah opened his eyes. "Yeah. And this is really important." He snapped the chair back into its nonreclining position, then leaned toward Fred, glancing furtively toward the stairwell. "Burwell is really bad with words," he whispered. "I mean, he mispronounces and misuses a lot of them. Sometimes, he just makes them up. Like he'll say 'dwelve' when he means 'delve.' Just try not to laugh when he does it, all right? I mean, I feel bad for the guy. He's gotta be allowed to hold on to his dignity. Whatever you do . . . don't laugh."

Fred just stared at him. Either Noah Percy was completely full of BS, or he was trying to play mind games. Maybe making up outrageous lies about a dorm adviser was some kind of weird boarding school hazing ritual. Not that Fred really cared. He just wanted to get this chair into his room.

"Hello?" a gruff voice called from the first floor.

Heavy footsteps began clomping up the spiral stairs.

Fred glanced toward the end of the hall. Maybe this was the "grotesquely fat" Mr. Burwell now.

A moment later, a middle-aged man in a dark,

double-breasted suit appeared out of the shadows. He looked as if he'd been up all night. Large purplish pouches hung below his eyes. His thinning brown hair was impeccably combed, but his flabby, grizzled face needed a shave. He didn't seem particularly happy, either. The downward arc of his lips suggested that he felt pretty much the same about the first day of school as Fred did.

He stared blankly at the chair.

"What the hell is going on here?" he demanded.

Before Fred could open his mouth, Noah hopped to his feet. "Uh . . . I can explain that, actually, Mr. Burwell," Noah said.

This is Mr. Burwell? Fred thought. No way. He wasn't all that fat. Well, he wasn't all that thin, either. But he hardly looked like a prep school "institution." He looked more like a strung-out boxing promoter, or a hit man in a Grade-B mob movie.

"See, Fred here doesn't have a chair," Noah continued. "So—"

"I know he doesn't have a chair, Percy," Mr. Burwell interrupted. "But I'm working on it. We just have to go through the proper channels."

"Uh . . . what do you mean?" Fred asked. He laughed, not sure whether Mr. Burwell was being serious or not. "What sort of channels does it take to get a desk chair?"

"Why don't *you* tell him, Percy?" Mr. Burwell said. His tone was menacing. His eyes shifted from the chair to Noah. "Why don't you tell your friend Wright here about the way things are done at the Wessex Academy?"

"What do you mean?" Noah asked.

"*You* tell *him*," Mr. Burwell said.

Fred glanced between the two of them. There was a weird dynamic here—one he wasn't quite understanding. Was Mr. Burwell angry? And why wasn't he speaking to Fred directly? And was buying a chair really that big a deal—considering he didn't even have one?

Mr. Burwell just kept staring at Noah.

A passage from *1984* floated through Fred's mind. He'd been thinking about that book a lot lately. Wessex had asked him to read it over the summer in preparation for a class called "Literature of the Twentieth Century"—but once he got into all the stuff about thought crime and Big Brother and Hate Week, he'd started wondering if there *was* actually such a class . . . if in fact the school just wanted to acquaint him with a brand of terror and repression that was similar to its own. Anyway, the passage was about a minor character, a servant named Martin, who'd had plastic surgery: "*a synthetic face was perhaps incapable of changing its expression.*" For some reason, Fred found that to be one of the creepiest parts of the whole book. Especially now. Mr. Burwell didn't appear to be angry. Maybe he *couldn't* appear to be angry.

"Tell your friend Wright here to read page fourteen of the orientation handbook," Burwell finally muttered. "The section on fire codes. Because if he reads that, he'll see that a chair like that has no business being in a dorm room. And he . . ."

He? He? Fred couldn't believe this. Mr. Burwell still hadn't introduced himself. He just kept talking about Fred in the third person, as if Fred wasn't even there. In fact, Mr. Burwell hadn't even *looked* at Fred yet. He'd only looked at Noah. But right at that moment—the very moment Fred snapped—the guy turned his beady eyes on him.

"Look, Wright, I know that you're new here. I know that you're supposed to be some hot-shot basketball star. But I also know how kids like you operate. You feel you have to break the rules. You feel like you have to impress guys like Percy by pulling some kind of outrageous stunt, like buying this chair. You play up this tough-guy, mah-koe, rebel image . . ."

Mah-koe?

Fred closed his mouth. Buying the chair wasn't an outrageous stunt; he had simply needed a place

44

to sit. But he forgot his annoyance. He stopped listening altogether. Mr. Burwell's fleshy lips were still moving—still spouting garbage about how the rules were in place for a reason, and how every item of furniture had to be provided by the school, but . . . but . . . *mah-koe*.

He *did* say "mah-koe." Didn't he?

Yes. Yes, he did.

And he must have meant . . . well, unless there was some word that Fred was unaware of, some other word pertaining to having a tough-guy image . . . but no. There *was* no other word.

Macho. That was it. *Mah-koe*.

So Noah hadn't been BS-ing. At least not about that.

"Just try not to laugh when he does it, all right? I mean, I feel bad for the guy. He's gotta be allowed to hold on to his dignity. Whatever you do . . . don't laugh."

Fred could feel a little tickle starting to well up in his stomach. It crept through his chest, forcing its way into his throat.

Mah-koe. Not *macho*.

He bit his lip.

Don't do it! he commanded himself. *Don't do it!*

" . . . the point is, a chair like that can block a quick exit," Mr. Burwell was saying. "Plus, with books and papers, you've got all sorts of insidiary materials. . . ."

"Ha!" Pent-up laughter exploded from Fred's lungs. *In-sidd-ee-ary.* He wasn't even sure what Mr. Burwell was trying to say. Incendiary?

"Wright!" Mr. Burwell barked.

"I'm sorry," Fred said.

"I'll bet you are." Mr. Burwell's eyes turned to ice. "You know what, Wright? I'm gonna say this once. Once only. There's three kids at this school who give me trouble up to here. And I'm not going to mention any names. I don't have to. Everybody knows it's Mackenzie Wilde, Hobson Crowe, and your new best friend, Noah Percy. So if I were you, I'd stay clear of them. Especially *him*." He jerked a finger at Noah. "Read the orientation handbook and—"

"I'm sorry, Mr. Burwell," Noah interrupted, holding up his hands. "You're right. This whole thing is my fault. But it's funny that you should mention the orientation handbook. Because just before you got here, Fred *was* reading it. Very diligently, I might add. And he had a question. Of a personal nature. Being as he's a new student and all, he wasn't sure how to tackle the subject. It's— um, well, it's uncomfortable."

Fred stopped laughing. He stared at Noah. What the hell was he talking about?

"What the hell are you talking about?" Mr. Burwell demanded.

"See, Fred told me that he's been wrestling with an issue on page thirty-eight," Noah said. He paused for a second, then laughed awkwardly. "He's a little embarrassed. It says there that your dorm advisers are your 'surrogate parents.' He . . . ah, he wants to know if that's meant to be taken literally."

"That book was written in nineteen sixty-two," Mr. Burwell said.

Noah shrugged. "I know. Look, what he really wants to know is if he can call you Dad."

Dad!? Fred stiffened.

"I mean, *I* think of you as Dad," Noah went on. "I always have. Ever since I was a freshman, I've felt an undeniable father–son connection between us. I feel I can talk to you about anything. Girls. Acne. College applications. The stock market. Those embarrassing moments in Comparative Religion when I've . . . you know, had an 'issue' with a pair of tight khakis . . . and had to stand up and give an oral presentation on Sufism."

Mr. Burwell blinked several times. His jaw tightened. Without another word, he turned and stomped back down the stairwell.

"I love you, Dad!" Noah called after him.

At that moment, Fred realized something. And it was kind of strange, because the realization was relatively trivial—at least compared to the possibility that he'd just witnessed the most freakish exchange of all time between a boy and a grown man. But it struck Fred nonetheless: This kid Noah had guts. He had a twisted sense of humor, sure, but he didn't take any crap. With one wacked-out rant, he'd not only stuck up for Fred, but he'd gotten rid of Mr. Burwell, as well. Too bad Mr. Burwell seemed like the kind of guy who held a grudge.

A door slammed downstairs.

Noah sighed. "Sometimes Dad and I have a hard time communicating," he said. "But I hear that's fairly common among single fathers and their troubled teenagers."

Noah Percy's Letter to Himself

Dear Noah,
How are you? I am fine. A word of advice for this
year: Don't obsess over Sunday Winthrop so much.
Frankly, it's pathetic. And yes, I know that a
conscious effort not to obsess is merely another
form of obsession—but you'll probably be more
comfortable with it, as you can pat yourself on
the back with little sayings like: "Man, I wonder
what I ever saw in that chick." Also, try not to
scratch your butt in public.

Yours, Noah

3

Noah Percy wasn't the kind of guy who feared being alone. Some people were scared of solitude—scared of being locked up in their own heads, with only their deranged thoughts to keep them company. Not Noah. He *enjoyed* the company of his deranged thoughts. Plus, he had the rest of the year to be around other people. He had no desire to join his friends, all of whom were watching their parents get drunk at Headmaster Olsen's house. Noah's own father was away on business in Zurich, meaning that it would be a mistake for Noah to go to the party. There was something undeniably sad about showing up at Olsen's on the first day of school, unchaperoned. Your alumni parents (or closest alumni relatives) validated your stature as an AB.

Without them, you were just another student—a waif, an orphan. And who really wants to be around an orphan?

Nobody. Right. So Noah chose to go to the Waldorf. It was a beautiful day, after all. He couldn't spend it holed up in his dorm with that new kid, Fred Wright. Besides, he'd nearly gotten a hernia helping to move that La-Z-Boy into Fred's room. . . .

The Waldorf wasn't a five-star hotel on Park Avenue. Well, it *was*—but this Waldorf was a clearing by a dry creek bed at the edge of campus, out in the middle of the woods. It was about thirty seconds from the nearest path and a good ten minutes from the nearest dorm. You pretty much had to know exactly where it was in order to find it. In other words, it was a sanctuary: a place to get away from the prying eyes of the Wessex faculty—to hang with your friends, to smoke if you were a smoker, to get busy with a significant other if you were lucky enough to be sexually involved, etcetera.

Noah was not a smoker. Nor was he sexually involved with anyone. The last time he'd kissed a girl was nine months ago—in his dorm room, on December 3rd, at 8:43 P.M. Her name was Darcy Black. She was a big girl. She sort of had a Tipper Gore-meets-NFL-linebacker vibe going. Noah made out with her for about twelve seconds. Then she told him that his breath smelled like cheese doodles, and left.

Being rebuffed by the likes of Darcy Black wasn't a real tragedy, though. Yes, it was humiliating—especially since she was later expelled for hacking into the school's alumni database and changing every name to Elmer Fudd. But it was also educational: Now he knew to brush his teeth more thoroughly after fatty snacks. Besides, what did he care about Darcy Black? Or anyone else, for that matter? Noah's heart belonged to Sunday Winthrop. And it always would, no matter how many letters he wrote to himself. The girl was . . . well, as Hobson Crowe would say, she was "mad phat stoopid fly, yo."

So—seeing as Noah was by himself and hopelessly in love with a girl who would never return his affections—he decided to do what any sexually frustrated boy would do.

He decided to build a fire.

Of course, he didn't actually intend to *light* it. That would be stupid, for a variety of reasons. On a practical level, lighting a fire at the Waldorf ran the risk of burning the entire forest down. On a more personal level, it was strictly prohibited by the orientation handbook (page fourteen, the section re:

fire codes)—and in fact could be punishable by dismissal. Still, Noah continued to gather dry twigs and arrange them in a neat little pyramid at the center of the clearing. Because it was fun to tempt fate, without really pushing it. Anyway, on the off chance he *did* change his mind, he doubted very seriously that he'd be expelled.

Example: Last fall, he'd tossed a firecracker into a toilet. On a whim. He hadn't really expected anything to happen. But the explosion had destroyed his dormitory's plumbing and bathed an exchange student named Sanjiv Desai (who'd had the misfortune of being in the adjoining stall at the time) in a shower of fecal matter. The poor kid ran screaming from the bathroom. Noah chased after him, apologizing profusely and offering to help clean him up—at which point the dorm adviser had apprehended Noah and hauled him into Headmaster Olsen's office. The ensuing interrogation marked the first and only time Noah had ever seen Olsen get angry. He kept fidgeting and stammering, and his face turned bright red.

"Wh-wh-why did you *do* it?" Olsen screamed.

Fortunately, Noah had prepared a cogent list of explanations. He still kept the list in his wallet, in fact, folded in a neat square right behind his platinum card.

Eight Reasons Why I Threw a Firecracker into the Toilet

by Noah Percy

1) I wanted to draw attention to myself.

2) An ignored ADHD diagnosis.

3) A manifestation of deep-seated frustrations with my emotionally retarded parents.

4) A manifestation of deep-seated frustrations with my status as a sixteen-year-old virgin.

5) My family is extremely wealthy and spoils me, so I can destroy material items without consequence.

6) I feel worthless much of the time, and vandalism gives me a fleeting sense of empowerment.

7) Blowing up a toilet *is* objectively funny.

8) Maybe somebody will put me in therapy now.

Upon reading the list, Headmaster Olsen had fallen into a kind of catatonic state. He gaped at Noah, but his eyes glazed over; he couldn't speak. He could only shake his head. In the end, he'd simply let Noah go with a warning and "probation"—a punishment so meaningless that it wasn't even defined in the orientation handbook. There was only one caveat: Noah's father had to pay for the plumbing repairs.

And that was pretty much the pattern when Noah caused trouble. Nothing happened. *Nada. Rien. Niente.* The faculty was simply too baffled by him to deal with his inane shenanigans in any constructive way. So were his parents. So was everybody else, for that matter. But Noah truly didn't mean any harm. He was just dealing with his myriad psychological issues by acting out—in much the same way he was doing now, by pretending to build this fire. Hey, at least he could analyze his own behavior. People should *all* be so in touch with themselves. Then the world would be a much saner place. . . .

There was some rustling in the leaves near the path. Noah quit the pretend fire-building and squinted through the tangle of tree branches. He heard the hushed sound of a girl's voice.

Sunday.

His insides clenched. He shook his head. Good God, he was a loser. With a capital *L*. Sunday Winthrop was a *friend*. A girl he'd met for the first time when he was four. Somehow, though, she had transformed into a goddess. He had no idea why. Maybe it had something to do with that long dark hair. She used to wear it in a preppy little bob, but then she grew it past her shoulders. She was more slender, too—slender and curvy . . . and her cheeks were always rosy. Aside from that, though, there was no rational explanation for the change in his opinion of her. None at all. So it was best just to try to not make a jackass of himself.

His eyes narrowed. Sunday was with Mackenzie and Allison. Nothing surprising there. But as they drew closer, ducking through the woods in their opening-day finery, he could see that Sunday and Allison were both wearing the exact same dress. And *that* was weird. As far as he could tell, girls usually went out of their way to avoid wearing the exact same dress.

Sunday was the first to reach the clearing.

"Don't mention the dress, Noah," she whispered.

He smiled. Interesting. Something weird *was* going on. "Oh, I'm fine, thanks, Sunday," he said. "How was the rest of your summer?"

She stuck her tongue out at him. She was so cute when she did that.

Mackenzie was next. "Oh—hey, Noah!" she called out in that sublimely ditzy voice of hers. "I was wondering where you were."

"Me, too," he said.

Then came Allison Scott. Noah opened his mouth to greet her, but quickly shut it. Allison's face was all red and puffy. Her eyes were bloodshot. Her mascara was running. He turned to Mackenzie and Sunday. Both of them seemed sheepish.

"Uh . . . Allison just dumped Hobson," Mackenzie

announced. "And she's all torn up about it. So if anyone asks, or if you hear any other kind of rumor—you know, that it happened the other way around . . . you heard the truth first. Right here."

Allison glared at her. Sunday looked as though she were trying not to laugh.

"Girls are so cool," Noah said.

"What's *that* supposed to mean?" Sunday asked.

"Well, it's totally obvious that Mackenzie is lying, that Hobson dumped Allison. No offense, Allison. But you all are sticking up for her. And sticking together." Noah nodded in approval. "Guys aren't like that. Guys love it when bad things happen to their friends. They never stick together. I mean, if you were a bunch of guys, you'd all be doing your best to make Allison feel like crap. You know, if Allison was a guy, too . . ." His voice trailed off. Everybody was staring at him. Judging from the look in Allison's eyes, she probably wished that she had one of her father's shotguns handy. "Don't worry; I'll go along with Mackenzie's story."

"That's not true," Mackenzie said.

"No, I promise," Noah insisted. "I won't tell anyone."

"No, no—not about that," she said. "About guys. Some guys *do* stick together. Like Winnie and Headmaster Olsen. They're in on this big secret—"

"Not the conspiracy theories again," Sunday groaned.

Mackenzie looked shocked. "What, you don't believe me?"

"Conspiracy theories?" Noah asked. "Cool. What are they?"

Sunday rolled her eyes. "Mackenzie thinks that Winnie and Olsen are in on an evil plot to take over the world. And Olsen's the leader. Doctor Evil."

Noah blinked. "Olsen?"

"That's right," Mackenzie said.

"Uh . . . we *are* talking about the same Olsen, aren't we?" Noah said. "The guy who hasn't changed his pants since the Reagan Administration?"

Mackenzie giggled, but she was struggling to be serious. "Just listen, okay? Sunday doesn't believe this, but earlier this summer, we ran into the Crowes and the Ellises out on Martha's Vineyard. And—"

"I have to side with Sunday on this," Noah interrupted. "You and the Crowes and the Ellises on the WASP resort island of Martha's Vineyard? That sounds *way* too far-fetched."

Sunday started cracking up.

Noah beamed, euphoric.

"No, no, no," Mackenzie said, shaking her head. "Just let me finish. See, we went to dinner with them, and Olsen suddenly showed up, too." She gave Noah a meaningful look. "And so we're all sitting around the patio of that lobster restaurant—you know, that place in Menemsha? And for some reason, Winnie and Olsen end up talking among themselves. And I hear them mention money." She raised her eyebrows. "See what I mean?"

"I . . . do," Noah said slowly.

Money. Right. Whew. Who *wouldn't* suspect an evil plot? Talk of money couldn't possibly be due to the fact that Olsen's primary job as headmaster was to *raise* money—and that Winnie's family was one of the wealthiest on the East Coast. Noah's dorm was *named* after the guy's family. He glanced at Sunday. Sunday shrugged. Noah had to shrug, too. Mackenzie was truly a wonder. If only he could glimpse reality from her point of view, just once. What would he see? Winnie and Olsen dressed in old-timey pirate costumes, burying treasure?

Well, actually . . . he *could* imagine Winnie doing something like that. The guy was a sociopath. Noah had had the bad luck of rooming with him freshman year. Winnie could quote almost any statistic imaginable on serial killers and horrible disasters, but claimed never to have finished an entire book. "I always know how things will end," he used to tell Noah cryptically, "and I never use *CliffsNotes*." He somehow always managed to get really good grades, too. And in spite of a hairy back and a penchant for overeating, he had a way with the ladies. (Not the

AB ladies, but *some* ladies.) Funny: The Marquis de Sade had a way with the ladies, too. So did mass-murderer Ted Bundy. *Hmm.* Mere coincidence? Mackenzie probably wouldn't think so. . . .

"What I want to know is, what was Olsen doing on Martha's Vineyard?" Sunday said. "Doesn't he usually summer in Nantucket?"

Mackenzie threw her hands up. "*That's* what I'm talking about! It's *weird.*"

"Yeah," Noah said. "I mean, it's not like he could have just hopped on a ferry—"

"Can everybody please just *shut up!*" Allison shrieked.

Whoops. Noah swallowed. Buzzkill. Everybody stared into space for a while. Oddly enough, this didn't ease the tension.

"So, Noah, how come you weren't at the party this afternoon?" Sunday asked quietly.

"Who *cares*?" Allison muttered.

Good answer. Before Noah could provide a rebuttal, however, he heard some more rustling out by the path. Maybe that was Winnie now, coming to dig a hole for his loot.

Yes. It was. But he wasn't alone.

Noah's eyes narrowed. The new kid, Fred, was with him.

Now *that* was weird.

Sunday and Mackenzie exchanged a confused

glance. Allison scowled. Noah felt a sinking feeling in his gut. Fred and Winnie picked their way through the tree branches, drawing closer and closer. Noah peeked at Allison again. She *hated* it when outsiders came to the Waldorf. Oh, boy. This could get ugly. . . .

"What's up, everyone?" Winnie said when he reached their little circle. "I thought I heard some voices out here."

"What's up, guys?" Noah replied, eyeing Sunday and Mackenzie—who now seemed even *more* confused. He was pretty confused himself. He turned back to Fred and Winnie. "Uh, when did you two meet?"

Fred and Winnie grinned at each other, as if reminded of an inside joke.

Allison's face soured.

"We're both on the basketball team," Winnie said.

"Oh," Noah said. Clearly, that wasn't the whole story. But for some reason, all the girls were staring at Noah now—as if *he* knew what was going on. "Um . . . everybody, this is Fred Wright. He lives in Ellis with me. He's a PG."

Fred's eyes narrowed. "A what?"

"A PG," Noah said. He tried to smile. "A postgraduate. We talk in shorthand here. You'll get used to it. Fred, this is Sunday, Mackenzie, and Allison. We're all ABs."

"ABs," Fred said blankly. "I won't ask." He nodded at the three of them. "Hey."

"Hey," Sunday said. "I think I heard your name mentioned earlier today." She smiled curiously. Noah frowned. Maybe *too* curiously—

"Hey," Mackenzie said.

Fred peered at Allison. "Did anybody ever tell you that you look just like Nicole Kid—"

"What the hell are you doing here?" Allison demanded.

Noah cringed. There it was: The Allison Scott Outburst. A Wessex perennial. He'd been expecting it, but it had actually taken a little longer than usual—almost ten seconds from initial contact with the undesirable element. Usually it took about three. Then again, she wasn't in top form. She was in pain over Hobson.

"Uh . . . just taking in the fresh country air," Fred said. He laughed. "Is there a problem?"

"Yes," Allison stated. "There is."

Oh, please, Noah thought.

Fred turned to Winnie, bewildered.

"Allison, just chill, all right?" Winnie muttered. "Fred wanted to see the campus. He's never even been to a boarding school before. I was giving him the grand tour." He arched his surgically enhanced eyebrows. "And I couldn't leave out the secret hot spots, could I?"

Aha. With that remark, Noah made the Fred–Winnie

connection: Fred must be a smoker. And he was Winnie's newest client.

Or victim, depending on how you looked at it.

For years now, Winnie had run a clandestine business out of his dorm room, selling cigarettes and chewing tobacco. Possession of any tobacco product or paraphernalia was punishable by suspension. But being an entrepreneur, Winnie decided to take all the risk upon himself and purchase the stuff for everyone else. He claimed he was doing the campus a favor. Kids no longer had to go to town to buy smokes, where they could be spotted by faculty members. They simply had to come to *him*. Dr. Feelgood. Needless to say, he also jacked up the price of the supply a little (what with the risk and all), making a tidy little profit. . . .

"Look, I'm sorry if I offended you," Fred said to Allison.

Mackenzie stepped forward and offered an apologetic smile. "No, no. It's—"

"Let me tell you something, okay?" Allison interrupted, fixing her cold eyes on Fred. "This is the Waldorf. You don't hang out at the Waldorf. You hang out at the Marriott. So just keep on sightseeing. You'll find it eventually."

Noah shook his head. Winnie rolled his eyes. Sunday and Mackenzie stared at their feet. They all knew why Allison was so pissed, of course. She firmly believed that the Waldorf was for ABs, and ABs only. The Marriott was for everyone else. It was so stupid. There was no difference between the two; the Marriott was just another clearing in the woods, on the other side of campus—and Fred had no way of knowing that, anyway. It wasn't the kind of information provided in the orientation handbook. But Noah was sure that Allison would give Fred a crash course in hotel hierarchy, and why it was so important to her. No doubt about it. Her three favorite topics of conversation were (1) herself, (2) herself, and (3) herself in relation to everyone else's social status.

"But the Marriott's all booked up," Fred said.

Noah laughed. Nice one.

"You don't even know what I'm talking about," Allison mumbled. "I'm out of here." Without another word, she brushed past him and stomped back toward the path, furiously swatting branches out of her way. Sunday and Mackenzie chased after her. Noah sighed. That darn girls-sticking-together thing. It always got in the way of a good time.

Fred watched them all go, an amused grin on his face.

"I'm really sorry about that, dude," Winnie said.

"Me, too," Noah added.

Fred just shrugged. He turned to Noah. "I bet she has a hard time communicating with *her* dad, too," he said.

Fred Wright's Dartboard

Dearest Diane,

I know that things are over between us, but I just
had to tell you something. Did you ever see the movie
AS GOOD AS IT GETS? It's with that fat old guy,
Jack Nicholson. Anyway, it was on TV the other day,
and there's this one scene where the main chick in
the movie, Helen Hunt, asks Jack Nicholson to give
her a compliment. Now, you got to understand: this is
one messed-up dude. He answers by saying that he
started taking medicine for his nervous tics.

And she's like, "How is that a compliment?"

And HE'S like, "Because you make me want to be
a better man."

Anyway, that's how I feel about you, Diane. That's
how I've always felt. You make me want to be a better
man. You make me want to deserve somebody like you.

Love always,

Sal

P.S. That guy you like from JERRY MAGUIRE,
Cuba What's-his-face, is in the movie, too.

4

"So . . . uh, I gotta ask you, man. And you know, don't take this the wrong way. But what *are* you doing out here? I mean, really. You're a smoker, right?"

Fred had to laugh. He was wondering when Noah would ask him why he was trespassing. It didn't take a genius to figure out that Noah was part of that girl's posse. And so this little secret hideout (*oooh—how exciting, a secret hideout called the Waldorf!*) obviously belonged to Noah, too. But at least Noah was polite enough to wait a good five minutes before posing the question. He'd even tried to make small talk. He'd explained what an AB was. An "Alumni Brat." That figured. From the little Fred had seen so far, the name definitely fit. These people actually dressed up to go to some hole in the woods.

"No, actually, I'm not a smoker," Fred said. "But I do enjoy a dip every now and then." He dug his hand into his jeans pocket and pulled out a small disc-shaped tin of Old Hickory Chewing Tobacco. "Want some?" he offered. He unscrewed the cap and took a pinch of the moist brown stuff, tucking it between his gum and lower lip.

"Oh, no, thanks," Noah answered. "I don't do the tobacco thing. You know, mouth cancer, lung cancer, heart disease, emphysema . . . uh, those run in my family. Plus, I don't like to support tobacco companies. They perpetuate a culture of addiction, while profiting from the labor of migrant workers. Statistics show that—"

"Spare him, Noah," Winnie groaned. "He's new."

"Right." Noah smiled. "Actually, dipping makes me barf."

Fred laughed again. "Yeah, it made me barf the first time I tried it, too. You just gotta get past it." The sweet, smoky flavor filled his mouth. Man, did he need this. He actually managed to relax a little. He hadn't thought that relaxing would be possible. His first day at Wessex had already been way, way too long—and it wasn't even over. Maybe he could just sleep out here. Anything to avoid going back to that cell. "So, anyway, to answer your question, I came here because Winnie told me that it was a good place to have a dip," he said.

Noah nodded. "I figured as much."

"I ran into him on the way into town," Winnie said. "I knew who he was, actually, because Olsen passed his picture around to everyone on the basketball team. So I came up to him, and right off the bat, he asked me where he could buy a tin of tobacco. Ballsy, huh? I could have been a narc. Anyway, I told him not to worry about a thing, to go back to his dorm. I'd take care of it." He grinned. "It was a fortuitous meeting."

Fred spit out a little glob of brown gook into the dirt. Yes, he supposed it was fortunate that he'd run into Winnie (even though the "ballsy" remark was a little too ingratiating), but that first part troubled him. Wasn't it kind of weird that the headmaster was showing off photos of Fred to his new teammates? It made Fred feel uncomfortable, as if he were being spied on or something. Maybe it just raised the specter of *1984* again—

"Oh, but dude, you know who I saw?" Winnie asked Noah excitedly. "That new English teacher, Miss Burke. Have you seen her yet?"

"Nope." Noah shook his head.

"She's the real deal," Winnie breathed. "Fresh out of college. She makes the talent around here look like a bunch of hags."

Noah glanced at Fred for confirmation.

Fred shrugged. He hadn't seen her yet, either. But he doubted she was *that* hot. She was a teacher. Which meant she was *older*. And as far as Fred was concerned, older meant lamer. Diane was older, too.

"Speaking of talent, what about that skinny chick with the long dark hair?" Fred asked. "The one who was just here. What's her name? Sunday? She's pretty hot." He sat cross-legged in the dirt, right next to a little tent-shaped pile of twigs. It looked as though somebody was planning on building a fire. Cool. That might be sort of fun. Like summer camp.

"Oh, no, I wouldn't mess with Sunday," Noah said, very seriously. "See, she was actually born a boy, but there was some hormonal imbalance, so she had to have a sex change. They say that some of her body parts . . . well, best not to go there. Also, her family has a history of schizophrenia, and her father is a drag queen. And I'm the only one who knows this stuff. So if I were you, I'd set my sights on somebody else."

Winnie laughed.

"Am I supposed to believe that?" Fred asked. "I mean, is that the truth?"

"I always tell the truth," Noah replied. For some reason, he spoke in a strange accent. It sounded vaguely Hispanic. "Even when I lie."

Fred stared at him, lost.

"That's a line from the movie *Scarface*," Winnie explained. "You know, that movie about the drug kingpin from the early eighties? Starring Al Pacino?"

"I don't think I've ever seen it," Fred said.

"Don't worry, you will," Noah said, switching back to his normal voice. "There's an unwritten rule at Wessex. Before graduation, every guy sees *Scarface*, and every girl sees *Grease*. You know . . . the musical?" Noah paused. "Never mind. Anyway, you'll hear a lot of lines from those movies around campus."

Fred blinked. He spit out another mouthful of brown gook. *Scarface* and *Grease*? What kind of school was this? Didn't they watch normal movies? He eyed the pile of twigs again. "Hey, Winnie, you got any matches?"

"Sure." Winnie dug into the pocket of his suit pants and tossed him a pack.

"What are you doing?" Noah asked nervously.

"Lighting a fire," Fred answered. He struck a match and dropped it onto the pile. The tiny flame sat there for a moment—then with a gust of wind it spread, dancing wildly. The twigs crackled and turned red. A wisp of smoke floated into the air.

"Hey!" Noah cried. "Don't do that! You could get expelled!"

Fred laughed. "It's just a little fire—"

"No, no, no!"

Noah jumped forward and stamped on the blaze with one foot, as if he were performing some kind of manic hoedown. Dirt and ashes flew everywhere. Fred tried to duck the fallout by scrambling away on all fours. He couldn't stop laughing.

"What's the big deal?" Fred asked.

"Nothing, nothing," Noah muttered. He slammed his foot down one last time. Black smoke billowed into his face. He coughed once. "It's just . . . I don't know. I mean, I didn't think anybody would actually *light* this thing—"

"Aw, look what you did, dude," Winnie grumbled. He was staring down at his legs. One of the glowing embers had landed in the cuff of his suit pants and burned a dime-sized hole in it. Fred could see the little horseman on Winnie's Polo sock. "Now I'm going to have to buy a new summer suit. Thanks, Noah. Thanks a lot. I'll catch you guys later."

"Sorry," Noah said.

"Hey, Winnie, wait!" Fred hopped to his feet. "Can I buy some more dip from you?"

Winnie reached into his inside jacket pocket and pulled out another tin of Old Hickory. "Five bucks," he said.

"But an hour ago it was *four* bucks," Fred protested.

"I was doing you a favor," Winnie said evenly. "I

do that for all my first-time customers. From now on, the going rate is five bucks."

"Are you serious?" Fred's smile began to fade.

Winnie raised one eyebrow. "I'm always serious when it comes to business," he said.

Fred stared at him, waiting for the punch-line. Then he sat back down in the dirt. Unbelievable. Clearly, this kid had watched one too many movies about drug kingpins. Did Winnie really think a cheesy cliché would convince Fred to overpay for some chewing tobacco? A tin of Old Hickory cost $3.50, tops.

"Never mind," he mumbled. "I'll go into town and buy it myself."

"Fine, if you want to take that risk," Winnie said. "But I've got to warn you, teachers are everywhere around here. They see everything." His tone hardened. "Especially in town. Especially if they know who to look for."

Who to look for? That sounded like a threat. A lot like a threat. Fred smiled again. "Are you saying that if I don't buy tobacco from you, you're going to rat me out to the teachers?"

"Did I say that?" Winnie glanced at Noah. But Noah didn't seem to be listening; he was trying to dust off his ash-stained pants. "Look, all I'm saying is that it's more risky buying tobacco in town than it is from me. Plus, you can have it right here, right now. You don't have to waste an hour walking back and forth from the drugstore."

Fred shook his head. The line sounded rehearsed—as if Winnie had said it a dozen times. He probably *had* said it a dozen times. He probably said it every time he convinced a new sucker to shell out five bucks for some Old Hickory. On principle, Fred didn't want to give in. On the other hand, he didn't want to be deprived of dip for the rest of the year, either. Whatever. In the long run, this was most likely a battle that wasn't worth fighting. And the walks to town *would* be a pain in the butt. Especially in the winter. He jammed his hand into his pocket and yanked out a crumpled five. "I'll take it," he grumbled.

"I knew you would. " Winnie snatched the bill from Fred's hand and dropped the tin into his lap. "You know where to find me." He turned back toward the path. "Logan Hall, room one-eleven. Noah can tell you where it is."

"Sorry again about the pants, Winnie!" Noah called after him.

Winnie didn't answer. He vanished into the trees.

"He's sort of a prick," Fred said in a thoughtful voice. He spit again.

"You haven't seen anything yet," Noah said. He kept vainly struggling to clean his khakis, but he kept spreading more of the charcoal around. "Winnie was indicted by the Securities Exchange Commission last year."

Fred's eyes narrowed. "Excuse me?"

"Yeah. He got involved in something called 'pump and dump.'"

"Pump and . . . *what*?"

Noah laughed. "Sounds kind of pornographic, doesn't it?" He finally gave up on his pants and sat down in the dirt. "It basically means buying a bunch of shares of some crap stock, then going on-line and chatting it up to a bunch of suckers on the Web, then selling it when the price shoots up. Winnie was really good at it. He made over a hundred grand. The story was actually in a couple of newspapers, although they never mentioned his name. He didn't even get in trouble with the school. He had to pay a big fine to the people he ripped off, but that was it. His dad donated a new science lab, so Winnie got off with 'secret probation,' which is total—"

He broke off in mid-sentence, looking toward the path.

Fred followed his eyes.

Some other guy was making his way to the Waldorf. He was tall, blond—suited up in a jacket and tie. Another perfect-looking preppy. Fred figured he had to be an AB, too. But something about him was slightly off-kilter. His pants were several sizes too big. They were pulled halfway down his butt. He slouched as he walked, in a pair of untied Timberland boots. He was also muttering to himself. It sounded like a drum beat: *"Boom cha, ba-boom-boom cha—boom cha, ba-boom-boom cha . . ."*

"Yo!" the kid said when he reached the clearing. He glanced at Fred.

"Hey, Hobson," Noah said. "Fred Wright, this is Hobson Crowe. Fred's a PG. He lives in Ellis with me."

"Wassup, dawg?" Hobson said. He bent down and extended a hand.

Fred shook it—and instantly found himself responding to a series of rapid-fire, thug-style hand-grips: the overhand thumb clasp, the slap, the finger-roll. Then the kid dipped in for a quick hug. Fred's jaw dropped. *What the—* But as soon as the procedure had started, it was over. Hobson stood up and slouched again, as if nothing had happened.

"You know where Allison's at?" he asked Noah.

"She was just here, ten minutes ago. What happened with you guys?"

"The girl's wack, yo." He glanced at the smoldering pile of twigs.

"Word," Noah said.

"I had to cut her loose. But she took it hard. I feel bad, yo. I didn't want it to be like that. I wanted to let her down nice and smooth. Know what I'm sayin'?"

"Word," Noah said.

"All right. I'm gonna see if I can find her." He took one more look at the ashes. "You know, y'all shouldn't kick it pyromania-style. That's guaranteed trouble." He flashed Fred a peace sign, then turned and headed back toward the path. "Peace out."

"Keep it real, Hobson!" Noah shouted.

Hobson laughed. He made an obscene gesture over his shoulder.

Fred watched the kid go, his mouth still hanging open.

That settled it. This place was a freaking lunatic asylum. He didn't know whether to laugh, or to be appalled, or what. Who *were* these people? White collar criminals and wanna-be gangstas and . . . he didn't even *know* what Noah was.

And the weirdest part about it was that they all looked exactly alike. They could have been cousins. Brothers, even. Didn't Wessex have any other types of students? The school brochure promised "a new era of diversity." But Fred hadn't seen a single black kid or Asian kid or Hispanic kid yet. Just a bunch of very strange white kids.

It was kind of frightening, in fact. Fred wasn't used to such homogeneity. Half of his old school was black or Hispanic. Fred's *best friend* was black: Jim Simmons, the other guard on the basketball team. Right now, Jim was at the University of Santa Cruz. Lucky bastard. But what would Jim have done if he had met Hobson Crowe? Actually, knowing Jim, he'd probably just laugh. He was about as much of a "homey" as Fred was himself. He watched *Buffy the Vampire Slayer* reruns. His favorite band was Matchbox Twenty.

"Hobson's on the list, by the way," Noah remarked, once they were alone again.

Fred turned to him. "What do you mean? He's an AB?"

"Yeah, but that's not what I mean. He's on Mr. Burwell's list of enemies."

"Mr. Burwell has a list. . . ."

Noah shrugged. "Well, it's not public or anything. But he resents a lot of the kids here. Especially the smart ones. See, he never wanted to be a math teacher. He wanted to write screenplays. Wessex was just supposed to be a stepping stone in his career. He wanted to be surrounded by a bunch of intellectual types for a year or two, because . . . you know, he isn't so good with words. But he only managed to write one feature. It was called *No More Scabs!* With an exclamation point. It was a romantic comedy about Jimmy Hoffa. You know, the old head of the Teamster Union who got messed up with the mafia and disappeared? Anyway, the script was rejected by everybody in Hollywood. Some studios even thought that Burwell was a student here, and that Wessex was one of those 'special' schools. That's why he's so bitter."

Fred laughed. He had to hand it to Noah: The guy's capacity for BS was astonishing. Did he just make this stuff up as he went along?

"Any more words of advice?" Fred asked dryly.

"Yeah—you like music?"

"Do I like . . . *music*?"

Noah nodded. "Yeah. What kind of music do you like?"

Shocking. This was actually a topic Fred could *understand*. A topic he genuinely cared about. It was *normal*. It was so normal, in fact, that he couldn't gather his thoughts; he was too frazzled. His brain swirled with the names of a dozen classic rock bands. "Uh . . . well . . ."

"Do you like hip-hop?"

"Uh, yeah. A little. But mostly—"

"Okay. You like hip-hop. Whatever. I mean, that's cool—I like the Beatles, myself, but most kids seem to like that rap stuff . . . anyway, my point is: Load up on a lot of obscure hip-hop CDs. Then go through them and make a list of all the samples. Then go out and buy *those* albums—the albums with the *original songs that are sampled*." Noah emphasized the last five words as if he were preaching the gospel. "That's deep, see. So people will come to your room—and by people, I mean girls—and they'll be like: 'Whoa. Who or what is Isaac Hayes?' And you'll be like: 'Oh, I saw that he was sampled by the Lost Boyz, so I had to get his record.' And they'll be like: 'Oh, my God. This guy is *so* deep. I *have* to have sex with him.'"

Fred smirked. "Really?" he said.

Noah nodded sagely. "Yup."

"Is that what that guy Hobson does?"

"You know it," Noah said. "And it works every time."

The sun had long since set by the time Fred got back to Ellis Hall, about a half hour before ten o'clock curfew. He was exhausted. Noah's chatter had worn him down as thoroughly as if Fred had played three hours of one-on-one basketball with him. And then there was also the overtime; Noah had talked incessantly during the entire walk home from the Waldorf—back through the lush woods . . . back past the playing fields and mansions and buildings that looked like Renaissance palaces.

Fred had tried to ignore Noah and focus on the crickets. He couldn't believe how loud the crickets were out here. This campus was nuts. There would never be a time when he wasn't blown away by it.

The library alone was the size of his old school—and Lincoln had three times as many students. The entire Wessex population, faculty and staff included, was less than four hundred. For all *this*.

"Good night, Fred," Noah said cheerily, slamming the door of his own luxurious room.

"Good night," Fred said.

He sighed. Now he had to go sleep on that stained mattress. In that *cell*. He hung his head as he rounded the spiral stairs up to the second floor. His footsteps were like lead. Maybe he could just spread his sheets and a comforter out on the La-Z-Boy. . . .

Oh, crap.

His door was open. The light was on. Perfect. First day of school, and somebody was already breaking into his room. He bolted down the hall—but the room was empty.

Fred hesitated in the doorway. His eyes widened.

The La-Z-Boy was gone. In its place was a metal folding chair. A copy of the orientation handbook lay on the seat.

And on the front cover, right on top of the photograph of Ellis Hall, was an oversized yellow Post-it note.

Wright:
I asked you to read the orientation handbook. In particular, the part about fire codes. Seeing

80

as you're new here, I'll give you the benefit of the doubt and assume you lost your copy. So here's a new one. I advise you to read it. It might interest you to know that lighting fires in the woods is against the rules, as is buying furniture that blocks exits, which I mentioned before.

Mr. Burwell

Part II:
Guerrilla Barbershop Quartet

Carter Boyce
Hadley Bryant
M. Hobson Crowe III
Chase Edward
** <u>Noah</u> <u>Percy</u>
Allison Scott
Boyce Sutton IV
Spencer Todd
Mackenzie Wilde
Sunday Winthrop

** Don't bother going through the time
capsule submissions. We should go with NP.
That slacker ennui is an act. So are the
lame jokes. He <u>loves</u> W. Even more than the
others, I'd say. Just like his father.
Definitely the best candidate so far. Also,
we should keep an eye on FW. He's a wild
card.

5

The next morning—for the very first time in her academic career—Sunday found herself in a strange mood. She was actually looking forward to the first day of classes. But then, about ninety percent of Sunday's waking life was spent looking forward to something in some way or another. Either she was looking forward to graduation, when she would be free from living at Wessex; or to college, when she would be free from the *kids* at Wessex (at least some of them); or to her glorious life *after* college, when she would be free from the prying eyes of anyone having to do with Wessex . . . because she would take her trust fund and flee to Bolivia.

But she never looked forward to class.

Unfortunately, however, classes provided the

only available excuse to get out of her suite. The suite itself wasn't a problem. It was spacious—the biggest suite on campus, in fact—and Sunday even had her own little bedroom within it. No, the *real* problem was that nobody had ever acknowledged that Allison Scott was seriously unbalanced.

Nobody ever talked about *anything*.

Maybe there was a solution to that problem, though. Sunday could call Mom and Dad and invite them to take a look at what Allison had done to their suite. Or rather, what Allison hadn't done (and what she had also prevented Mackenzie and Sunday from doing)—which was unpack. Sunday's toiletries and bras and framed pictures were still in a suitcase. She hated that, the feeling of being unsettled. But in the wake of Hobson and Allison's breakup, Allison had announced that she was going to focus all her energies on "female bonding again, spending time with friends." And the first step in the bonding process was to make the suite "a real home."

So she'd hired an interior decorator.

Now, last night, when Sunday was told that a twenty-eight-year-old gay Swede named Sven Larsen would be driving up from New York City on Thursday to pick an "aura" for their bedrooms, she had not seen it as cause to celebrate female bonding. Nor did it help matters when Allison showed her an article in *Marie Claire* about Sven Larsen, featuring a self-portrait—bald and unsmiling in a black kimono—and citing his numerous awards for an "austere approach to design: interiors where stark absences and a lack of softness define the mood."

Okay. First things first. Sunday did not need an "aura" for her room. She was a senior at a boarding school. Not a neurotic yuppie. There was plenty of time for that later. And her mood was fragile enough without being defined by "stark absences." Plus, she *liked* softness. If she wanted a few throw pillows and stuffed animals on her bed, then dammit, she would have them.

But once again, Mackenzie stepped in on Allison's behalf—and after much prodding (and gentle reminders that Allison *was* going through a hard time), Mackenzie got Sunday to agree to let the esteemed Mr. Larsen at least take a peek at her little bedroom. After all, Allison was paying for the whole thing. And if Sunday didn't appreciate Sven Larsen's vision, she could always go back to decorating her own personal area herself.

"Who knows?" Mackenzie had asked her earlier, over a bowl of granola at the dining hall. "Maybe you'll end up being a lot happier without so much clutter."

Sure I will.

The long and the short of it was this: Sunday was

going to spend a lot more time in the library, at the Waldorf, and involved with extracurricular activities. If Mackenzie wanted to indulge Allison, fine. But Sunday wasn't going to be a part of it. No, sir. She was no baby-sitter. She was a clutter-and-softness kind of girl, all the way.

At least, that was what she'd told herself at breakfast.

By the time third period rolled around, however, Sven Larsen's ideas on clutter were sounding better and better. Sunday's *brain* was cluttered, and lunch was still a good hour away. As usual, a summer of sunning and sailing had wiped her brain clean of any memories of actual class time. And now she had to subject herself to College Algebra. Yikes.

Math had never been Sunday's strong suit. Particularly if it was being taught by Mr. Burwell. But she had to fulfill the math requirement in order to graduate, and College Algebra certainly seemed preferable to Calculus—especially since that calculus book was so damn big. Still . . . she just couldn't handle math today. It was too much, too soon. So when she slumped into a spot at the back of the classroom, she was determined to give herself a break. She would float off into space for the next fifty minutes, and really pay attention tomorrow. . . .

But then that kid appeared. Noah's housemate. Fred.

Sunday couldn't help staring at him.

He marched into the room—no, he *swaggered* into the room—ignoring all the curious glances . . . as if he'd been at Wessex his entire life, as if he were an AB himself. And those clothes. She could already spot three glaring dress code violations: jeans (boys were supposed to wear either khakis or cords to class), some kind of bizarre Central American-style neo-hippie sash threaded through his belt loops (boys were required to wear belts), and sneakers (not allowed).

She had to hand it to him. Fashion statements like that took guts.

The thing about him, though, was . . . he wasn't *cute*. At least not in the conventional way. Then again, which way was "conventional"? He was a little on the skinny side, but he was tall and dark, with broad, square shoulders. He had nice eyes, too—a kind of deep, chocolate brown. He was a hell of a lot better looking than someone like, say, Winslow Ellis. But she could just imagine what would happen if she presented the two of them before her parents and asked them to choose:

Mom: "This Fred looks anorexic."
Dad: "Winnie's operation truly worked wonders, hon."
Mom: "Exactly. Besides, Winnie's healthy. We know his family."

Dad: "Good point. Do you know anything about this Fred's past?"

Mom: "Just look at that thing around his waist. It's the most awful thing I've ever seen."

Dad: "That's a sharp blazer, Winnie. Is that a Paul Smith?"

Fred's gaze swept the room, searching for an empty seat. He began making his way down the aisle. Sunday stared down at her notebook. There was an empty seat right beside her. There was *always* an empty seat right beside Sunday—unless there was another AB in the class.

Fred took the seat.

He looked over at Sunday and smiled. "Hey," he said.

Sunday swallowed. "Hey," she said.

Mr. Burwell walked in and slammed the door. Today's double-breasted suit was beige. She'd never seen that one before. He must have done some shopping over the summer. He took off the jacket and draped it carefully over the back of a chair, then immediately started talking. About what, however, Sunday hadn't the faintest clue. He might as well have been speaking in Swahili. *Blah, blah, blah.* She couldn't focus on anything but Fred. She could feel his eyes on her. What was he *doing*? Well, he was probably checking her out. That was what boys did, wasn't it? Yes. She'd been checked out this summer, too, on the beach, by guys who didn't know her—normal teenage guys. Like Fred. But it was just so . . . strange. It had been so long since anyone *here* had mustered the courage to check her out (at least in an obvious way) because Wessex was so repressed and because people thought she was a prude. . . .

A crumpled wad of paper plopped on her desk. From *him*.

She tried not to smile. A note. *Everybody* was staring at her now. They all saw it. Perfect. It was so deliciously seventh grade. A tingle shot through her body. Ahh, seventh grade. The year of romance! The year she kissed Chase Edward in the boathouse of the West Egg Yacht Club, and nearly fainted with pleasure! (Chase Edward still made her ill, but that was another story.) She stole a quick sidelong glance at Fred. He was staring straight ahead at Mr. Burwell, pretending to hang on the guy's every word. Amazing. A writer *and* an actor—a Renaissance man. She slid the note into her lap and unfolded it.

Hi. I'm Fred. We met yesterday, remember? Anyway, I just wanted to ask you if you know where to get a good chair around here. My room didn't come with one, and Mr. Burwell—who I understand is a "Wessex Institution"—stole mine. It was a real beauty, too. A genuine La-Z-Boy.

Sunday allowed herself a little grin. She didn't know quite what to make of this. On first read, it seemed like the kind of nonsensical gibberish that Noah Percy would write. On the other hand, there was a certain humor to it. And the ironic tone was undeniably flirtatious. Yes. He was trying to impress her with charm and wit. Maybe it wasn't poetry, but still . . . a decent first effort, all in all. She turned the scrap over and scribbled a hasty reply:

Why would Mr. Burwell steal your La-Z-Boy? Do you two have some kind of relationship I should know about?

She surreptitiously tossed the note back at him. It bounced onto his notebook. Fred didn't even bat an eyelash. He was cool under pressure, this one. He waited the obligatory five seconds or so before sweeping it into his lap—then a smile spread across his face. He wrote his own reply below hers and lobbed it back.

Yes, Burwell and I are in the midst of a lovers' quarrel. Well, either that or I'm on his enemies list. But that's not the reason he took my chair. Somebody else took my chair out of my room before I even got to school, and for some reason Burwell insists that I go "through the proper channels" to get a new one. Maybe you can tell me why.

Oh, my God.

Sunday nearly burst out laughing. It couldn't be . . . but it *had* to be. Fred lived in Ellis Hall. Her father's chair had been *found* in Ellis Hall. Sunday turned to him.

"Do you live in room two-oh-three?" she mouthed silently.

His eyes narrowed. "What?"

"Two-oh-three?" she whispered.

He nodded. "Why?"

She bit her lip, then shot a quick glance up at the front of the classroom. Mr. Burwell was writing something on the board. "I have your chair," she murmured.

"You *what*?"

She shook her head, struggling not to laugh. "It would take too long to explain."

Fred smirked and pointed at the note. "Oh, no. You have to explain. Write it down. If I'm gonna have to spend the rest of the year hunching over—"

"Wright!"

Sunday winced.

Mr. Burwell wasn't writing on the board anymore. He was huffing down the aisle, his eyes wide.

"What are you two doing down here?" he demanded, looming over them. He stood with his stomach thrust forward. Not a good call. His blue shirt was stretched tautly over his gut. Little football-shaped mounds of white flab suddenly appeared between the buttons, running in a zipperlike pattern from the middle of his chest right down to his belt. He should have known better than to stand that way; he was a math teacher, and this was a fundamental matter of mathematics. There was too much gut and too little shirt.

"I was trying to talk to Sunday," Fred said.

Sunday smiled in spite of herself.

Mr. Burwell's face reddened. His eyes flashed between the two of them. Suddenly, his chubby hand darted out like a frog's tongue and snatched up the note from Sunday's desk.

Her jaw dropped. *No, no, no—*

"'Yes, Burwell and I are in the midst of a lovers' quarrel,'" Mr. Burwell read aloud. He spoke in a monotone. "'Well, either that or I'm on his enemies list . . .'" He stopped and looked at Fred. "You and I aren't in the midst of a lovers' quarrel," he said. He laughed. It sounded like a backfiring lawnmower engine: *Pah!* "From what I can tell, the only lovers here are you and your little pen pal, Miss Winthorp."

A couple of kids snickered.

Sunday slumped in her chair. Slowly, the color drained from her face. Well. *This* was certainly an interesting way to kick off senior year. Talk about humiliating. She could see the future very clearly now. Oh, yes. It didn't take a consultation with Mackenzie's star charts. Nope. The moment the bell rang, everybody in this classroom would run out and tell all their friends that Sunday Winthrop was hot-and-heavy with Fred Wright. A PG. A one-year student, a non-AB. A jock. The lowest of the low. Mr. Burwell had all but confirmed it.

What a hypocrite, they were sure to say. *She acts like a snob and a prude, but she's already got something going with some meathead. . . .*

She glanced over at Fred.

He was glaring at Mr. Burwell.

"Why did you steal my chair?" Fred suddenly demanded.

"Excuse me?"

"You heard me," Fred said.

"I didn't steal anything," Mr. Burwell replied. He crumpled the note and shoved it into his jacket pocket, then turned and marched back to the front of the class. "Now, let's get back to mathematics. That's what we're here for."

"Are you saying you didn't take it?" Fred cried. "Then what happened to it? You know, I paid for that with my own money, and I—"

"You should have read the orientation handbook

before you spent that money," Mr. Burwell interrupted.

All at once, Sunday was consumed with anger. *Good for you, Fred,* she thought. He was standing up to Burwell. He had the right idea. *She* should be pissed, too. She should also be challenging that fat fool. The stolen chair, the public shame . . . all of it was an injustice. And screw everybody else. What did she care if people spread rumors about her?

But as soon as these thoughts raced through her mind, she could feel herself clenching up. Yes, she was angry. But she *did* care about the rumors. Because she knew exactly what would happen. She would be sent to Headmaster Olsen's office. Then Headmaster Olsen would call her parents. Then her parents would forbid her to associate with "this Fred." And then Mom and Dad would have their various minions—Olsen, Allison, Winnie, Mackenzie (although Mackenzie would refuse to spy and be really psyched for Sunday)—keep an eye on her for them. The surveillance team was in place. Mom and Dad had used it before. It was ridiculous: Sunday didn't even *know* Fred, but any chance of getting to know him better had already been quashed.

" . . . you have no right to accuse me of anything," Burwell was saying to Fred. "You and Miss Winthorp were passing notes and—"

Enough.

"It's Win-*throp*," Sunday snapped. "Not Winthorp. You know, this is my fourth year at this school, and the *third* class I've taken with you . . . and you still haven't learned to pronounce my name right." She glared up at him. "How would you like it if I called you Mr. Bur-*will*? Or Mr. Bur-*wall*? Huh?"

His lips tightened. He thrust a finger toward the door. "That's it," he hissed. "Headmaster Olsen's office. Right now."

"Fine."

For an instant, she felt wonderfully empowered.

Then the feeling swirled down the drain. Sighing, she gathered up her belongings and headed for the door.

"And don't look so sorry for yourself," Mr. Burwell called after her. "That's the way the ball crumbles when you cause trouble."

Sunday rolled her eyes as she sauntered into the hall. *That's the way the ball crumbles when you cause trouble.* Now *that* was a classic "Burwellism." Over the summer, she'd forgotten about Burwellisms: those bizarre, fortune-cookie-like pronouncements that confounded everyone at Wessex, faculty and administration included. (Best one ever: "In my day, it was the ceiling, the floor, and your butt crack.")

Noah Percy actually kept a running list of Burwellisms. He said he was planning to carve them all in a monument that he would build in Burwell's honor upon graduation. Sunday couldn't wait to see how long the list was. Ten pages, at least. That was her bet.

Of course, being confronted with a Burwellism was a little bittersweet, because it marked one of those rare occasions when Sunday actually felt bad for her parents. Tuition was $25,000 a year. For *him*. How had the guy even been hired? His only skill was making people feel bad about themselves. At the very least, Wessex could afford to provide him with a book of clichés and quotes—so he could study how they were properly phrased, so he wouldn't always get them mixed up. It would probably save everyone a lot of embarrassment.

Mackenzie Wilde's anonymous contribution to the Wessex "time capsule"

I'm still not sure why they picked me to contribute something for this. I never get picked for anything. I'm the black sheep of my family. Not that I mind. Every family has to have one black sheep, right? Anyhoo, when did black sheep get such a bad rap? I mean, I've never actually seen a black sheep in real life, but I imagine if I did, he or she would probably be really, really cute. We have a black Lab named Buster, and *he's* cute. Black looks good on animals. It never goes out of style.

I bet black is still in style twenty-five years from now. Am I right?

So, I guess I should tell you a little about myself. Without giving myself away. That's hard! This is supposed to be anonymous. Maybe I should start with what other people say about me. Some say that I act and talk like a five-year-old. I think that's because I have a high-pitched voice. Also, certain unnamed people at Wessex have told me that I'm flighty (yes, to my face, can you believe that?)—but I later found out that those people are Aries and Scorpios, so I forgive them. Aries and Scorpios have the hardest time dealing with their own aggressions. I should know. I'm a Scorpio myself. Not that I'm very aggressive. I mean, sort of.

I guess I do have a hard time concentrating on one subject for very long. But that makes sense, given my PLH (Past Life History). Janis Joplin couldn't concentrate on one thing for very long, either. They say now that she probably would have been diagnosed with Attention Deficit Disorder as a kid, if they had known what it was back then.

This summer, I got way into exploring my PLH. I found this book on past life regression therapy at a flea market in Edgartown, on Martha's Vineyard. It's called *Past Life Regression Therapy*. There's another part of the title, too—a sexier part, like "Meet the Marie Antoinette in *Your* Past." I think that's what it is. Anyway, it's this really cool how-to book that teaches you to hypnotize people and call forth all these repressed memories from their past lives, memories that help them deal with their problems today. It was only three bucks!!!

Like, for instance, before I read it, I had no idea why I was so obsessed with the number twenty-seven. I mean, I would count to twenty-seven all the time. I found out that it was exactly twenty-seven steps from my bedroom to the kitchen. I was also totally convinced—and still am, actually—that I was going to die a tragic death right before my twenty-eighth birthday. But then I found out that I was Janis in a past life, and she died a tragic death when *she* was twenty-seven. Isn't that crazy? It makes perfect sense.

By the way, I swear I'm not trying to brag or anything by saying that I am the reincarnation of Janis Joplin. If you read the book, you'll find out that *everybody* has at least one famous person in their PLH. Some people even have more. That's what's so cool. Maybe whoever's reading this has a famous person from my time in *their* PLH. Makes you think, doesn't it?

Anyway, I want to get Allison and Sunday (those are my two best friends) to agree to let me hypnotize them. Especially Allison. Well, Sunday, too. But I know that digging up some stuff from Allison's PLH will help her get through this bad patch with Hobson. Maybe it will even help them get back together. There's no harm trying, right? (Mental note: Ask Hobson if he also wants to be hypnotized.) And Sunday seems so sad all the time, even though she tries not to show it. I bet something really heartbreaking happened to her hundreds of years ago—like she lost her sailor husband at sea, or she was forced to flee the hut she'd lived in for forty years when Genghis Khan attacked.

But mostly, I want to explore their PLHs to get to the bottom of this communication problem that they've been having. I mean, there's *no* good reason—*none at all*—why Allison and Sunday shouldn't be as close as they were when we were all little kids. Astrologically, they're a perfect match. Sunday's a Sagittarius with Capricorn rising; Allison's a Leo with a Taurus rising. So they're both fire signs. (Fire does best with fire.) And they both thrive on being the life of the party, the center of the action. They're both generous. And they're both honest. They both tend to live in the moment.

See what I mean? It's like . . . duh. Given *those* circumstances, they should pretty much be in love. Plus, they were both born at the tail end of Pluto in Libra, which means that they seek harmony and compatibility. And still, they can't seem to see things eye-to-eye. So I wouldn't be surprised at all if they were trapped in a weird triangle of betrayal in their past lives. You know, some kind of thing where, like, Sunday was Bathsheba and Allison was King David's wife or something.

It wouldn't even bother me so much if I didn't feel like I was caught in the middle. It's not bad when I'm able to work things out between the two of them, but sometimes it kind of sucks. Especially now, since Allison's boyfriend, Hobson, dumped her, she just hasn't been herself. She's been in such a crappy mood. She's even been *mean* to me. Like, I mentioned the whole concept of past life regression to her, and she just gave me this look, and then said, "You know, the only reason you're at Wessex is because your Dad donated the new observatory."

Ouch. Sure, I know I'm not going to win any genius awards. But does she have to rub it in? Enough people do that already. Sunday's running out of patience with Allison, too. And who can blame her? After all, some Swedish guy is coming up to make her take all her pictures off her wall.

But Sunday's so awesome. I mean, she always tries her best.

It's so weird, though—because in the same way that Sunday and Allison *should* be so tight, Sunday and I *shouldn't*. Like I said, I'm a Scorpio, and everybody knows how Sagittarians tend to leave Scorpios in the dust. And when I really think about it, the only thing we have in common is that we both like sexy dancing.

But that's the magic of it. Sometimes the stars can't tell you what to do. We're just lucky. Especially since Sunday's last name begins with the same two letters as mine. We always get to sit next to each other whenever seating arrangements are alphabetical.

The only thing I *can't* stand is that Sunday doesn't believe me about the stuff I overheard this summer: the conspiracy stuff. I've got to get her to see the truth. That's my second mission, after getting Sunday and Allison back to where they belong, relationship-wise. I just know that Olsen and Winnie are up to something no good. I still haven't put all the pieces in place yet, but they're out there. All I need is the proof.

Anyway, I guess I should end this with my hopes for what will happen twenty-five years from now. Here's what they are:

1) Hobson and Allison will be married, and one of their kids will be reading this.

2) Winnie and Olsen will be in prison, serving time for their yet-to-be-determined but most definitely heinous crimes.

3) I will defy the odds and live beyond the age of twenty-seven.

4) Sunday will find true happiness.

I think I'm in love.

Until this very moment, Mackenzie Wilde had never considered herself same-sex oriented. Okay, sure, it wasn't as if she'd ever ruled out experimenting or anything. She just hadn't had the opportunity. And, yes, there also was that time when she'd convinced herself that she had a crush on the lead singer of No Doubt . . . what was her name? Gwen Stefani. Right. But that was just a lapse of reason. That hadn't lasted any longer than a week. This was different. This was the real deal.

Mackenzie slumped back in her chair and gazed up at Miss Burke. She couldn't put her finger on *why* she found Miss Burke so attractive, so strangely compelling. It was just one of those cases—well, to

quote an old saying (and Mackenzie never understood why those old sayings got such a bad reputation, anyway)—where the sum of the parts was
greater than the whole.

Or was it the other way around?

The whole was greater than the sum. . . . She
could never remember how it went.

Oh, well. It didn't matter. Because when Mackenzie
really dissected it, she saw that Miss Burke had *every-*
thing going for her. The parts *and* the whole. She was
a brand-new teacher—a breath of fresh air in the
stale, stodgy old Wessex fog. And she was just
twenty-two years old, barely five years older than
Mackenzie—young enough to be a sister . . . a *friend*,
even. And she was beautiful: delicate and petite,
with greenish eyes and Snow White ivory skin and a
long mane of black hair.

But the coolest thing about her was the way
she'd introduced herself to the class. *"Hi. My name is*
Miss Burke. I'll be exploring twentieth-century literature with
you for the next three months. And just so you know, I also
teach modern dance. Anybody interested in modern dance can
see me after class. I'm a vegetarian, too. So if I catch anyone
eating a Slim Jim in here, you'd better watch out!" It was so
funny. Even thinking about it made Mackenzie
smile. . . .

"Yes?"

Mackenzie blinked.

Miss Burke was staring at her, eyebrows raised.

Blood rushed to Mackenzie's face. *Uh-oh.* She glanced around her little row—at Noah, at Allison, at Winslow Ellis. They were all staring at her, too.

"Do you have a question?" Miss Burke asked.

"Uh . . . what? I mean, no—no I don't," Mackenzie stammered. She struggled to sit up straight. The wooden chair screeched on the floor. "Sorry, I was . . ."

"Exploring the final frontier?" Miss Burke finished with a wry smile. "Don't worry. Spacing out is perfectly understandable, especially on the first day of classes. You're still in summer mode. I was just worried I had a crumb on my face or something."

A couple of kids in different rows chuckled.

Mackenzie just smiled up at her. Wow. Smart, funny, beautiful, *and* super-nice.

"Speaking of summer, let's move on to the summer reading, shall we?" Miss Burke said, adopting a more serious tone. She leaned against the wall by the chalkboard. Her eyes roved over the classroom. "Let's see . . . summer reading . . ."

Summer reading. Mackenzie's pulse picked up a beat. Damn. She *knew* there was something she forgot. And chances were that she hadn't already read the book on the list, not unless it happened to be

Past Life Regression Therapy. Maybe? Nah. That wasn't really a Wessex kind of assignment.

"How about you?" Thankfully, Miss Burke zeroed in on Noah. "The young man in the tweed jacket."

"Me?" Noah asked.

Miss Burke nodded. "Yes. What were your first impressions of *1984*? Tell me anything. Just off the top of your head."

Noah cleared his throat. "Well, to be honest, Miss Burke, I . . . uh, I was a little delinquent when it came to reading that particular book. I mean, I could go off and BS, and make up some lie—like, oh, wow, I really liked the part about Big Brother, you know . . . But I don't think that would be fair to either of us. Do you?"

Miss Burke didn't respond.

Mackenzie swallowed. She could feel her face getting hot. *Not good.* She had a very, very bad feeling that Noah was about to launch into one of his comedy routines.

But then Miss Burke smiled. "What's your name?"

"Noah. Noah Percy."

"I see. Well, I certainly appreciate your honesty, Noah. And you're absolutely right: Your lying to me wouldn't be fair to either of us. But tell me—if you don't mind my asking—why *didn't* you do the required summer reading?"

He sighed. "Well, I didn't really have time."

"Oh, no? Busy vacation?"

"Yes. Thanks for asking." He gazed up at her as if he were falling into some kind of weird trance. "I was very busy. I felt I really needed to spend my time getting back in touch with an old friend." His voice softened. "An old friend named Noah."

Miss Burke burst out laughing.

Whoa. Mackenzie sure didn't see *that* one coming. A teacher thought Noah was *funny.* That was a first in Wessex history. And Noah *was* funny, of course (he was a Scorpio, too, after all), but his sense of humor was . . . well, Mackenzie actually didn't know *what* it was, other than strange. Even Noah himself seemed a little surprised.

"Excuse me," Miss Burke said. "Sorry. You just sort of caught me off guard there, Noah. But I think I can forgive your delinquency, provided you read the book this week." She cocked her eyebrow to let him know she wasn't kidding. "And as a matter of fact, your comment was representative of a trend that started in the wake of such books as *1984.* Can you tell me what that trend is, Noah?"

He hesitated. "Uh . . . postmodernism?" he said.

Miss Burke's face lit up. "*Very* good," she murmured. She turned to the board—but not before giving Noah an appreciative little glance.

Mackenzie sagged in her chair. How did Noah do it? One second, he was pissing off Miss Burke; the next, he was her prize student. Well, he was funny. And smart. Yup. That's what it took: smarts. And a lot of reading. *Hmm*. Maybe she could ask Noah to suggest some books for her to read . . . in, like, a really informal kind of way, just to give her a boost. . . .

"Psst." Allison nudged her.

"What's up?" Mackenzie whispered.

Allison pointed furiously at Miss Burke as she scrawled on the chalkboard. "Can you believe that?" she hissed.

"Believe what?"

"How *inappropriate* that was," Allison muttered, scowling. She shook her head and glared at Miss Burke's rump. "I mean, what was that *look* she just gave Noah?"

Mackenzie shrugged. She sat up straight in an anxious effort to appear as if she were actually paying attention.

"Come *on*," Allison growled between tightly-clenched teeth. "I mean, who does she think she is? She waltzes onto this campus, coming from some hippy-dippy college where they probably run around naked half the time, and she has no idea of the Wessex tradition—"

"Yes?" Miss Burke asked, glancing over her

shoulder. She scanned the room. "Would some-body like to add something?"

Please, Al, just be quiet, Mackenzie silently begged. The last thing she needed was to be busted for day-dreaming again. She kept her eyes squarely focused on the blackboard.

POSTMODERNISM: A MOVEMEN

Miss Burke went back to writing. Mackenzie exhaled. She could actually learn something here. This was *important.* So why was Allison getting so mad? And why did she always get so hung up on little phrases like "Wessex tradition"? Mackenzie didn't even know what that *meant.* It was best just to ignore Allison right now. Yes. It pained Mackenzie, but this was for Allison's own good. The girl was obviously still completely hung up on Hobson, and she was using her own depression as an excuse to lash out at everyone around her. . . .

Allison nudged Winslow Ellis.

Out of the corner of her eye, Mackenzie watched as Allison leaned over and scribbled something in Winnie's notebook:

I can't believe this woman. She calls herself a teacher? Olsen is going

*to hear about this at the first student
council dinner. That's for damn sure.*

Luckily, Winnie just laughed. "Miss Burke
probably will, too," he whispered. "She's the new
faculty adviser, along with Mr. Burwell."

Mackenzie smiled. Now *that* was some good news.

Allison folded her arms across her chest and
sulked.

Oh, my God!

Something else on the page caught Mackenzie's
eye. She *knew* it. Yes. Conspiracy! And here was the
proof she'd been looking for. In the upper right
hand corner of his notebook, Winnie had written
the following message to himself:

TALK TO OLSEN AT 3:30 TODAY ABOUT NEW AGENDA.

Well. If that didn't spell "foul play," Mackenzie
didn't know *what* did. She couldn't wait to tell
Sunday about this.

Allison Scott's List of Grievances Against Miss Burke (for personal purposes only)

1) She barely looks old enough to drive.

2) All the boys are practically slobbering over her.

3) She's not even pretty, unless you like low-class, junkie types.

4) That professional academic act she's putting on . . . what a phony!

5) I found out she went to Wesleyan. Is that even an accredited college?

List #2 (for Headmaster Olsen's eyes only)

1) She made suggestive gestures toward a male student.

2) She did not discuss the summer reading (not in depth, anyway).

3) She allows students to lead the direction of classroom discussions. (No syllabus.)

4) Inappropriate wardrobe.

5) She discussed personal matters (i.e., she's a vegetarian, and she also teaches dance).

7

" . . . . really, Sunday. I know it's difficult to settle back into the school routine after a summer of relaxation, but this kind of behavior is simply not *fitting* for a student of your stature, and I feel that . . ."

Sunday could feel her eyelids getting heavy. Olsen's lectures always had that effect on her. He was like a hypnotist. No, actually, he was more like a very powerful sleeping pill. One of those prescription-only medications. A single dose of his rambling monologue—and *pow!* You'd be knocked cold for at least twelve hours, the potency further enhanced by his soporific leather couch (a great word, "soporific," she'd learned it meant "sleep-inducing" while taking an SAT course last year). . . .

"So do you see my point?" he asked.

"Huh?"

Sunday struggled to sit up straight. Unfortunately, the cushions were a little too slippery. She nearly fell onto the floor.

Olsen peered at her over the rims of his spectacles. "Methinks the lady doth not listen," he said with a wry grin.

"Methinks," Sunday groaned silently. That was another thing she'd conveniently forgotten over the summer: Olsen's bizarre fondness for Shakespearean language.

"Sunday, please," he said. He leaned across the desktop and clasped his hands in front of him. "I can't stress how important it is that you buckle down. It's time to get serious about academics. Fall trimester of your senior year is *the* trimester that counts. Colleges are paying attention to your every move. You do understand that, don't you?"

She nodded. Her eyes darted to the grandfather clock in the corner. Eleven twenty-five? Jesus. She'd only been in here five minutes? That clinched it: This office definitely occupied some weird zone in space where time slowed to a crawl. . . .

"This is *important*, Sunday," Olsen stated. His jowls wriggled. His jowls always wriggled when he tried to be stern. It was sad, in a way. Even in a full-fledged rage, he was about as intimidating as

Barney the Dinosaur. "What would your parents think if they knew you were passing notes to some boy in class? If they knew you were being disrespectful to Mr. Burwell?"

"Disrespectful to Burwell?" she cried. Suddenly she was wide awake and filled with righteous indignation. "Excuse me, Headmaster Olsen. The man doesn't even know my *name*. I mean, how does somebody who is so . . . so . . ." She was too flustered to continue. Olsen *had* to threaten her with tattling to Mom and Dad. It was so . . . predictable.

"Mr. Burwell is an esteemed member of the Wessex faculty," Olsen said. He sounded as if he were reading a blurb off a cue card. "He is a top-notch math teacher, a superb wrestling coach, a fine dorm adviser—"

"Come *on*," Sunday interrupted, unable to control herself. "Top-notch math teacher? He once said, 'Ninety-nine times out of ten, somebody wins in the game of football.' If that's top notch, I should think about transferring to Carnegie Mansion."

Olsen's face darkened.

"Okay, okay . . . sorry," Sunday said. "Look, can we just speak honestly to each other here?" She shifted in her seat. The cushions kept making obscene-sounding squishy noises. "I mean, you're friends with my parents—"

"I will not have you talking about a member of

the faculty that way, Sunday," Olsen stated. His jowls started wriggling violently. They looked like they had reached a dangerous critical mass, like they might explode in a deluge of all the vodka and cocktail wieners Olsen had consumed over the last thirty years. "It is completely inappropriate. And frankly, my relationship with your parents doesn't change the fact that I'm your headmaster. You can't go on acting this way, unless you want real trouble."

Sunday sank back into the couch. Real trouble? Funny. She already *had* real trouble. This whole mess was going to come up in a conversation with Mom and Dad. She knew it. So whatever punishment Olsen wanted to give her—Sunday detention (actually fairly enjoyable; it just meant sitting in the library all day and reading); dining-hall cleanup (kind of yucky, but it provided unlimited free access to candy bars); or "conservation crew" (clearing paths through the woods with the maintenance guys, some of whom were pretty cute)—it didn't matter. It was small potatoes. Because people would be watching her now. Questioning her. Judging her. Reporting back to Mom and Dad via the AB network. . . .

"Sunday?"

She glanced up at him.

His face softened.

"Yes?" she mumbled.

"Listen. Let's just put this unpleasantness behind us, shall we?" He leaned back and smiled, then adjusted his spectacles. "Let's look to the future. Speaking of which, you are going to join us for the student council dinner a week from Saturday, aren't you?"

Oh, God. The student council . . . now, if anything truly crystallized how little control she had over her own life, it was her membership on the student council.

She didn't *choose* to be on it. She hadn't *run* for it. And she certainly didn't care about the rules it presumed to uphold. Yet last year (at her parents' request, no doubt, even though they denied any involvement) Olsen had appointed her as "social coordinator." Just like that. Out of the blue. He hadn't asked her if she'd wanted to join; he'd simply created a position for her—and usurped another four hours a week of potential freedom in the process.

The title meant nothing, of course. It *was* nothing. The only thing she'd ever done was plan a juniors-only dance. And the dance had never happened. The DJ who was supposed to perform—some sketchy platinum-dye-job named DJ Wack MC—had been arrested the previous night for selling Ecstasy at Carnegie Mansion, when he'd played *there.* And still, Sunday kept her position. It was ridiculous. All she had to her credit was one utter failure. But did that matter? Apparently not.

The most absurd part of all was that there were plenty of kids at Wessex who would *kill* to be on the student council. Like this one girl, Kate Ramsey. She wasn't an AB, but she'd run for treasurer every single year. But so had Winslow Ellis. And every single year, Winnie somehow managed to squeak by with a victory. The look on Kate's face when she heard those results, again and again and again . . . well you wouldn't think that she'd lost an election. You'd think her puppy had died. It made Sunday sick, now that she really thought about it. Why couldn't Olsen create positions for the Kate Ramseys of the world? *They* were they ones who deserved the breaks.

"Sunday?" Olsen prodded. "The dinner?"

"You know what?" Sunday said. She pushed herself out of the couch and stood. "I don't think I'm going to make it. I think I'm going to resign."

"Excuse me?"

"I just don't have an interest in being on the student council anymore," she said.

For a few seconds, he just stared up at her. He looked as if he'd been slapped. His jowls were perfectly still. "Sunday, I don't—"

"Really, Headmaster Olsen," she interrupted gently. She offered a rueful smile. "I'm sorry. It's just the way I feel. Why don't you pick somebody else to be the social coordinator? How about Kate Ramsey? I bet she'd be great—"

"Listen, Sunday, please, I know you're upset. But let's try not to—"

"What's the matter with Kate Ramsey?" Sunday asked.

He blinked several times and averted his eyes. "Well. Well—nothing, of course," he stammered. "It's just . . . ah, I mean, we have a certain dynamic on the council that's already in place . . . and bringing somebody new in now—before elections, I mean, you know . . . it just might complicate things a little. We already have a new faculty adviser. Miss Burke. Besides, as I said earlier, this is a crucial time in your life. Colleges are watching. Being a council member isn't just good for Wessex, it's good for your future. . . ."

Ah, yes. The future. Sunday could see what was happening here. Olsen wasn't particularly concerned about Sunday's future. Well, he was—but he was much more concerned about his own. He was concerned that he might be *blamed* for Sunday's resignation. If Sunday started mouthing off to teachers and dropping extracurriculars—well, then, her parents would look to Olsen for answers. Why couldn't he talk some sense into her? What was his failing? And maybe, just maybe, if he didn't have the answers to those questions . . . Mom and Dad might just be a little more stingy with their donations.

Now she felt guilty. She didn't want to put the guy in a bad position. He'd spent his entire life kissing the behinds of people who gave the school money, *fretting* over their behinds. And one little move on Sunday's part could topple a whole row of dominos—triggering accusations, bad karma, and possibly an ulcer. Sunday turned to the door. All right. Olsen *was* very kind to her. He'd gone out of his way to procure her father's chair for her, after all. Sure, that was strange. It might even qualify as deluded. But the intention was nice.

"Sunday?"

"Don't worry," she said. "I'll be at the dinner."

He sighed. "I'm very glad to hear that. But there's still the matter of—"

"Speaking of the future, can I ask you something?" Sunday interrupted. For some reason, she had a sudden, terrible suspicion that Olsen had read what she'd submitted for the time capsule. "Um . . . you don't open people's time capsule submissions, do you?"

Olsen sat up straight. He seemed genuinely taken aback. "Of *course* not," he breathed. "That would compromise the integrity of the whole exercise. We want students to feel free to write whatever they want, to say whatever they feel. That way the students of the future will get a real, objective, unbiased look at what's going on here today. You've seen how it's done. You give us what you write in sealed envelopes, and then we bury them intact. And even if we *did* read them, we wouldn't know who—"

"Okay. Thanks." She smiled, reassured, then reached for the doorknob. "I'm kind of late for my next class, Headmaster Olsen. I'll see—"

"There's still the matter of Mr. Burwell, Sunday. I'd like you to write a formal apology. A letter. More than one line, too. A real—"

"Okay, Headmaster Olsen. I will. Bye."

Sunday slammed the door behind her. The sound echoed down the long stone hall. She closed her eyes and exhaled. At least she was out of there. Now she just had to flee the building. She hated this place. Whoever had designed the Wessex Administration Headquarters must have taken a cue from the architects of Nazi Germany. High ceilings, drab gray marble—

"Are you all right?"

Sunday's eyes popped open.

It was Fred. He was sitting on the wooden bench right outside Olsen's office.

"Uh, yeah," she said, puzzled. "What are you doing here? Did Mr. Burwell send you to see Olsen, too?"

"Nope." Fred shook his head. "I just came here to wait for you."

All at once, Sunday's face felt hot. "Uh . . . why would you do that?" she asked.

"Because I'm bored," he said simply. "Nobody does anything around here. I mean, I thought boarding school was gonna be all about food fights and pep rallies and sneaking off campus to get wasted. But here, everybody just sits around and *talks*. I could've stayed at home to do that."

She laughed. "Well, why don't you do something about it?"

"Funny you should mention that," he said. "That's actually the real reason why I came. I got you in trouble. I want to do something to make up for it."

"Like what?"

He shrugged. "Whatever you think is right."

"Don't worry about it." She began a hasty march toward the exit.

Fred jumped up and followed close on her heels. "No, really, I'm serious," he insisted. "It'll help us get past this whole chair problem. I got you in trouble—"

"But I didn't *get* in trouble," she said. She walked a little faster, just to make sure Fred couldn't get in front of her, so he couldn't see the idiotic grin that had inexplicably formed on her face. Her footsteps clattered on the stone. "I never get in trouble."

"Oh, no?" He laughed. "What's your secret?"

She paused, taking a moment to get herself under

control, then turned to him. "My secret is that I agree to go to stupid dinners at Headmaster Olsen's house. I agree to meet with other members of the student council. I agree to eat a really nice meal while we all pat each other on the back and talk about how great we are."

"You wanna run that by me again?"

"Not particularly," she muttered.

"Can I join the student council?" he asked.

She shook her head and continued toward the door. "I doubt it."

"Why not?"

"You're not an AB," she said simply.

"Oh. Okay. That's cool. Well, look. I came all the way over here to say I'm sorry. The least you can do is come have a dip with me."

Her face reddened. "What?"

"A dip. A little pinch of chewing tobacco."

She looked down at the floor as she walked. Her long black hair fell across her eyes. "No, I . . . uh, I don't do that."

"Well, then, show me where the Marriott is," he said. "I'm sick of dipping alone."

She stopped and turned, shocked. "You haven't found the Marriott yet?"

Fred smiled. "Nope. And I have to find someplace else to dip soon. No offense, but the Waldorf bums me out."

Sunday shook her head, flustered. "Well, some-body else could show you where—"

"Who?" He laughed. "I don't have any friends."

"But . . . but how—what about Winnie?" she stammered.

"He's not my friend. He just wanted to make a buck by selling me dip and showing me where to chew it. I mean, I'm glad he did. But people like that, you know, they're never really your *friends.* They just want something from you. They're usually pretty phony."

Sunday stared at him. She grinned again. She knew she must have looked like a fool, but she couldn't help herself. For some reason, that astute observation sent the same tingle shooting down her spine as his first note had. Weird. There was no logic to it. Objectively, Fred was just an overgrown PG with a skinny frame and a lousy wardrobe. He was a sharp PG, sure—but still, any PG was wrong for her. *She* was an AB. *She* never associ-ated with anyone outside the circle.

"Fine," she heard herself say. The words seemed to tumble out of her mouth of their own accord. "I'll take you to the Marriott. But if you're as bored as you say you are, you have to promise me you'll do some-thing to liven up the action there. You can't just sit around and talk. You've got to make a move."

Fred nodded back. "Deal," he said.

Carter Boyce
Hadley Bryant
M. Hobson Crowe III
Chase Edward
** <u>Noah</u> <u>Percy</u>
Allison Scott
Boyce Sutton IV
Spencer Todd
Mackenzie Wilde
Sunday Winthrop

** Don't bother going through the time
capsule submissions. We should go with NP.
That slacker ennui is an act. So are the
lame jokes. He <u>loves</u> W. Even more than the
others, I'd say. Just like his father.
Definitely the best candidate so far. Also,
we should keep an eye on FW. He's a wild
card.

- - - - - - - - - - - - - - - -

Agreed. I'll make the necessary
arrangements. The PBs are confirmed for
Phase One. We'll set this year's asking
price at $200K. And don't worry about FW.
He'll fall into line soon enough.

8

Fred tried to play it cool as Sunday led him through campus, ducking into an uphill path that started in a heavily wooded area right behind the Arts Center. In truth, he was a little anxious. His heart thumped. He was sweating. He probably smelled. He didn't even trust himself to speak. The last words she'd said kept reverberating through his head, over and over—like the annoying buzz of an alarm clock:

"You've got to make a move."

What the hell did that mean? All right, he could guess what it meant. Which was the first good reason not to do it. Never do the expected.

Or *did* it mean that? He'd thought that Sunday was supposed to be some kind of prude. That's what Noah had told him last night. Well, Noah had also told him

that Sunday was a hermaphrodite, a Satanist, a canni-
bal, and an evil Soviet superbaby planted in America
during the height of the Cold War.

Obviously, Noah had a thing for her. Which was
the *second* good reason not to make said "move." He
didn't want to get in the way of Noah's action.
Because in spite of the kid's strangeness, he was
probably the closest thing to a friend Fred had at this
place. And Fred didn't really want to interfere with
that. He had to admit it: He *liked* Noah. So far, Noah
appeared to be the only person at Wessex who didn't
seem to want anything from him.

But the first good reason not to make a move
(and the best reason, of course) was that Fred hadn't
made a move in over a year. He was a little out of
practice. Yeah, sure, he'd told himself that he was
over Diane. That he was ready to get back at her.
That he was primed to scam on zillions of easy prep
school chicks in a frenzy of meaningless sex. . . .

"You don't talk much, do you?" Sunday asked.

"Huh?" He glanced up from the trail. "I just—"

His toe struck a root. He went staggering into
her. But in the split second before impact, he
decided not to use his hands to break his fall; she
might get the wrong idea—so his nose slammed into
her shoulder. He caught a whiff of that pleasant,
lemony, sweater-smell. . . .

"Hey!" She propped him up. "Easy there. Guess you're not much of an outdoorsman."

Oh, brother. He wondered if his face looked as hot as it felt. He straightened and stepped away from her, smoothing out his rumpled clothing. "Actually, I went to a camp where they taught survival skills," he grumbled. Then he felt like punching himself. What the hell was *that*? Yes, he'd learned survival skills—but now he sounded like some disturbed twelve-year-old camping geek who read *Soldier of Fortune* magazine. "So, uh, where is this place, anyway? I have class fifth period."

"So?" Sunday snickered. "I have class right now."

"You do?"

"Yup. Art History." She shrugged, then turned and kept walking. They were almost at the top of the hill. "To be honest, I was sort of looking for an excuse to blow it off."

He grinned. "Um . . . am I missing something here? Can people just blow off class? Or is that just an AB thing?"

"Depends who the teacher is," she answered matter-of-factly. "If the teacher reports it to Olsen, you get Sunday detention. If he doesn't, then you're off the hook. And it doesn't matter if you're an AB or not. Certain teachers are just lazier than others." She glanced over her shoulder. "You'll figure it out."

"Oh." Fred watched her as she pushed some branches aside. Then she veered off the path and disappeared over the hillside.

He shook his head. Somehow, in the last ten minutes, the tables had been turned. Before this moment, he felt in control. Well, all right—not really *in control*. But at least he'd been relaxed. Funny. On point. But now, suddenly, *she* was all of those things. And he was . . . what? A twelve-year-old camping geek? What had happened?

By the time he caught up with Sunday, she was closing in on a clearing—a clearing that was actually bigger and tidier than the Waldorf. It even had furniture: two rusty metal chairs.

One chair was occupied by a pale girl dressed all in black: long black skirt, black sweater, black boots. She had dyed black hair and a silver nose-ring. She was puffing on a cigarette. The other chair was occupied by a short redheaded guy with freckles. He was staring off into space. Neither of them looked particularly happy.

"*Voila*," Sunday announced. "The Marriott."

An odd wave of both relief and disappointment rushed over Fred. Sunday had probably known that there would be other people out here. Sure she had. So "making a move" hadn't meant . . . well, *making a move*.

Hmm. Probably a good thing. Wasn't it?

The Goth girl and the redheaded guy stared at Fred and Sunday.

Fred wasn't sure what to do. All he wanted was a dip. He'd be happy to have one right where he was standing. He didn't want to barge in on anything.

Then Sunday waved.

The girl frowned. She glanced at the guy, as if to ask: *"What the hell is Sunday doing here?"* But the guy wasn't looking at Sunday. He was looking at Fred.

Sunday approached. Fred figured he'd better follow. The redhead's eyes hardened as Fred drew closer.

"Hey," the kid growled. "You're Fred Wright, aren't you?"

"Uh, yeah," Fred answered tentatively.

"I'm Tony Viverito," the kid barked. "That name ring any bells?"

Viverito. Jesus. Yes, that name *did* ring some bells. Some very sour, off-key bells. So. Diane's boyfriend Salvatore had a little brother. It figured.

"They didn't mention Tony Viverito to you?" the kid demanded.

"No," Fred murmured. "Hey, look, I don't know what—"

"Tony Viverito." All of a sudden, the kid exploded with a stream of expletives so vile that Fred was actually repulsed; he couldn't help but subconsciously bleep them out, like a TV censor: "I was starting [*bleep*]-ing point guard last year. I was supposed to start this year. That is, until that [*bleep, bleep*], Coach Watts, told me that some [*bleep*] PG from some [*bleep*] would [*bleep*] me out and take my position. Still doesn't ring any [*bleep*]-ing bells?"

Fred sighed. So *that* was the problem. In a way, he was relieved. At first, he'd thought Tony was pissed because Fred had dated his brother's girlfriend. But no. Tony Viverito just happened to be the kid whose position Fred had unwittingly swiped. It was still an unpleasant coincidence, of course, but at least it had nothing to do with any personal vendetta.

"Hey, man, I'm sorry if I messed up your plans," Fred said. "I'm just trying to get into college, you know?"

The kid laughed. "Get into college? Yeah, I was hoping to get into college, too. Dartmouth, actually. But it's gonna be a lot harder getting into Dartmouth now that I've been benched. Basketball was the one thing I was good at. Now I don't have that anymore. So, yeah, you could say you messed up my plans—"

"Lay off, Tony," Sunday groaned. "Fred didn't take your spot on *purpose*. So he happens to be a better basketball player than you. So what? Colleges aren't gonna *know* that. All they're gonna see is 'Varsity Basketball' on your application."

"Shut up, Sunday," Tony muttered.

Sunday just laughed, though. "If you're so worried about Dartmouth, why don't you try out for the drama club? Do something besides sports. Join the Wiff 'n' Poofs or something—"

"That's easy for you to say," the girl interrupted. "You don't have to do *anything*. Your family probably *owns* half of Dartmouth."

"Yeah," Tony said. "You can go to college wherever you want."

"Yeah," the girl added. "You're probably gonna be initiated into some secret society, like that movie, *The Skulls*, or whatever."

"Yeah," Tony said. "You and the rest of your AB posse are gonna control our lives forever—"

"Hey, hey, hey!" Fred yelled. "Shut up!"

Everybody glared at him.

"Sorry." He offered a smile. He dug into his pocket and yanked out a tin of Old Hickory, then held it out to Tony and the girl. "Look, why don't we all just have a dip and chill out, okay?"

"I don't dip," Tony muttered. "It makes me barf."

"Me, too," the girl said. She glared at Fred, angrily puffing on her cigarette.

Fred shrugged. "Fine. That's fine." He took a deep breath, then shoved the tobacco back in his pocket. "All right. Listen. I'm new here. I'm still getting used to things. So I don't know about these little cliques you have, these *AB*s or *PG*s or whatever other kinds of abbreviations you use—"

"Pags," the girl said, exhaling a cloud of smoke.

Fred paused. "What's that?"

"Pags," the girl repeated. "Park Avenue Granola Sluts. You know, those pseudo-hippie chicks who dance around campus listening to sixties rock, pretending to be these free and easy age-of-Aquarius throwbacks—but who really live in penthouse apartments on Park Avenue." She sounded as if she were talking about war criminals. "PAGS."

Fred's smile soured. That description came pretty close to Diane. Frighteningly close, in fact. Except for the slut part. Well, maybe that, too. But he forced his lips back into their upright and locked position. This wasn't about Diane. He didn't *care* about Diane. This wasn't even about Salvatore Viverito. No. This was about breaking down social barriers. After all, Tony wasn't the same person as his brother. *He* didn't steal Diane. He was just a guy. Right. He might even be a *cool* guy, for all Fred knew. Very suddenly, Fred felt as if he were on a mission. He was going to . . . *make a move.*

"The point is," he said, "I don't know an AB from a—"

"Then why are you hanging out with *her*?" Tony

demanded, jerking a finger at Sunday. Fred shrugged. "It just happened, man. I don't know. She's in one of my classes. Why does anybody hang out with anybody?"

The girl snorted, then stubbed her cigarette out under a black boot. "Gimme a break."

"You wanna know the truth? I met Sunday in the woods. At the Waldorf. Just like I'm meeting you now." Fred took three quick steps across the clearing and extended a hand to the girl. "Fred Wright. What's your name?"

The girl just stared at him.

"Fred Wright," he repeated.

Finally, she took his hand. Hers was moist and limp. She wore a silver ring on every finger. "Sarah Mullins," she said.

"Excellent. Nice to meet you, Sarah Mullins. You, too, Tony Viverito." Fred stepped back. "Now I'd like you both to stand up."

Sarah and Tony exchanged a blank glance.

"I'm serious," Fred insisted. "I'd like us all to form a little circle." He turned to Sunday. She was staring at him with a look that could best be described as horror. "Come on. I just want to show you something."

Nobody moved.

"Come *on*," he urged. "I'm not gonna bite you or anything. Look, what's the worst that can happen? I give you this little demonstration, and you go back and tell all your friends that some PG freak named Fred made you do this weird thing at the Marriott—and it'll provide a lot of great dining hall conversation. At my expense."

Sarah and Tony exchanged another glance, but this time Sarah smiled.

"Come on, come on . . ."

Slowly, they pushed themselves out of their seats and stood. Fred's heart started thumping again. Strange: At this moment, he felt more alive than he ever had at Wessex so far. And he had no idea what the hell he was doing. He waved Sunday over. She shrugged, sort of hopelessly, then joined the three of them in a circle.

Fred nodded. "Good," he said.

"What *is* this?" Sunday asked.

He took another deep breath. "I want to show you something here. The argument we just had should prove something to us. We're all in the same boat. We're all freaking out about colleges. We have a lot more in common than we don't. We're all *the same*. I mean, really. We all like to hang out in the woods, right? And Sarah and I use tobacco products. Tony and I both play basketball. See what I mean?"

Nobody said a word.

He looked from face to face. It was like looking at a police line-up—or a photo array of people who all suffered some terrible discomfort, like chronic constipation or hemorrhoids.

"But for some reason, we don't *trust* each other," he forced himself to continue. "We all have these ideas and hang-ups and whatever, and we've made judgments." He smiled at Sunday. "Now, as I was telling Sunday a few minutes ago, I went to this summer camp. And the very first thing they made us do there was stand in a circle with a bunch of strangers. We did this thing called trust falls. Any of you know what a trust fall is?"

Sunday shook her head.

So did Sarah.

"You're a freak, dude," Tony said.

"Well, I'll show you what it is," Fred said. He positioned himself so that he was standing about three feet from Sunday, with his back to her. Then he closed his eyes and raised his arms. "I'm gonna fall backward right now. I'm putting all my trust in Sunday. If she doesn't catch me, I'm gonna hit the ground. It's gonna hurt." He paused. The wind rustled his hair. It smelled of cigarette smoke. "Ready, Sunday?"

"Fred, I don't—"

"Ready?"

"Come on, Fred. This might—"

"Three . . . two . . . one . . ." He held his breath and allowed his body to go slack. He pitched backward, fully relaxed. His head spun. *Uh-oh—*

"Whoa!" Sunday cried.

Her hands dug into his armpits. The two of them went stumbling backward. But Sunday prevailed. She didn't let him drop. After a second of teetering around in her arms (yes, this was the closest he came to making a move, and it actually felt pretty nice), he opened his eyes, then removed himself from her grip.

"See what I mean?" he asked everyone. He grinned and straightened himself out.

Sunday smiled shyly.

Sarah looked awed. Well, either awed or frightened. She started clapping.

"Did I mention that you were a freak?" Tony asked.

Fred gestured to Sunday. "Now I *trust* her, see? She saved me from certain doom. And once we go around, and everybody saves everybody else, we'll all have reached a new understanding. We won't be ABs or PGs or PAGS or any of it. We'll just be a bunch of kids having some good, clean fun in the woods. Huh? Huh?"

Tony rolled his eyes. "I'm outta here," he grumbled. He stalked off toward the path.

But Sarah was laughing. She started clapping again. "Come on, Tony," she called. "Just hang out for a sec. This could be fun."

"Can't do it," he answered, without bothering to

turn around. "I have English next period. With that new teacher, Miss Burke. And I can't be late for *that*. 'Cause she is one fine specimen of womanhood. . . ." He whistled and disappeared over the hilltop.

Sarah frowned. She shrugged and turned to Fred. "Whatever."

Fred felt a brief pang of guilt. But he brushed it aside. He shouldn't worry about Tony. Anyway, Sunday was right: He hadn't taken Tony's spot on the team on purpose.

"All right," he said. "We can do it without him, anyway. Sunday, you're next. Sarah, you be her spotter."

The two girls jumped into position. And around the circle they went—Sunday into Sarah's arms, Sarah into Fred's arms . . . and with each successive fall, the laughter and clapping grew louder and louder. The guilt over Tony faded. *Yes*, Fred thought. This was deep. This was *profound*. It didn't take a four-year student to understand the significance of this moment. Oh, no. That a girl like Sunday was actually communicating with a girl like Sarah—*everybody* could understand that. It was the rarest of the rare: a connection between a preppy and a Goth rocker. Fred felt a rush of adrenaline he hadn't felt since . . . Jesus. Well, since he'd won the regional championship at Lincoln. It was the feeling of power. Of *triumph*.

And right at that moment, he had an epiphany.

He'd been fooling himself until now. He kept telling himself that he would *use* Wessex, that he'd be the outsider. But no. That wouldn't be his thing. His thing would be to turn this place around. To bring people together. Like that song by the Youngbloods, the one Diane loved so much: *"Come on people, now, smile on your brother . . . everybody get together, try to love one another right now."* Yes! He would be a sixties-style Pied Piper of love and harmony! No more ABs! No more PAGS! No more abbreviations of any kind!

Mr. Positive. That was the new Fred. He'd bury the bitterness over Diane, too. Why drive himself crazy over her? She'd moved on. He should, too. This afternoon, he'd take the first step. He'd throw out Salvatore's letter: a symbolic and practical gesture, rolled into one. Then he'd make friends with Tony. Yes. They would become *great* friends, in fact. And Tony would invite him over to the Viverito house for a long weekend, and he would sit around the dinner table with the Viverito brothers . . . and Diane would be there, too—and she'd see what a great guy Fred had become, and they'd start playing footsie under the table. . . .

"Fred?"

Sunday was standing with her back to him, arms outstretched.

"Want to go the other direction?" she asked.

He raised a finger. "In a sec," he said. He stroked his chin.

Sunday turned to him. Sarah gazing at him now, too. Expectant. Focused. Waiting for another burst of wisdom.

"You know, I was just thinking," Fred said. "Everybody here uses abbreviations for everything. But you guys left out the most obvious one of all."

"Which one is that?" Sunday asked.

"Boarding school," Fred said. He was beaming. "BS."

Their faces all melted in wide-eyed astonishment, as if Fred had just delivered the Eleventh Commandment.

"Of course," Sunday said.

"Wicked," Sarah said.

"It's time to take the BS out of boarding school!" Fred cried.

They burst into applause.

Fred took a bow. Yet as he did, a thought occurred to him. His triumph was incomplete. He needed to make amends with Tony Viverito. He needed to prove to the guy that he wasn't out to screw anyone over. He was just here . . . well, because for whatever bizarre reason, fate had brought him to Wessex. And from now on, he was going to make the most of it.

Sunday Winthrop's Formal Letter of Apology to Mr. Burwell

Ms. Sunday Winthrop
Reed Hall #301
225 South Chapel Street
New Farmington, CT 06744

Mr. Paul Burwell
Ellis Hall Apt #1
44 Kendall Lane
New Farmington, CT 06744

Dear Mr. Burwell,

I am very, very, very, very, very, very, very, very, very, very, very sorry I was so impudent in class this morning.

Sincerely,
Sunday Winthrop

P.S. You'll notice this letter is more than one line.

Noah Percy's Top Five Burwellisms

1) "Don't you dare look at me with that tone of voice."

2) "Ninety-nine times out of ten, somebody wins in the game of football."

3) "I'm not saying anything. I'm just saying it's ironical."

4) "Turkey? Ha! Next you'll tell me there's a country called Pig or Cow."

*5) Burwell: "You know what your problem is, Percy? You think too much. Don't think."

Percy: "So how should I solve this problem?"

Burwell: "I don't know. What do you think?"

*This last one is not a Burwellism in the true sense, but still makes the list for so successfully embodying the spirit of Burwellisms.

9

"So?" Olsen demanded. He leered at Noah across the wide expanse of the desk. "What do you have to say for yourself?"

It was definitely a new record: Noah had survived *six* straight periods without being sent to Olsen's office. And he would have survived the entire day, too, if it hadn't been for one stupid little joke he'd made in Modern European History. The joke hadn't even been offensive, at least not in the classic Noah Percy style—the *modus operandi* that was both so oddly self-conscious and disrespectful that a person couldn't help but freak out. No. This had just been a moronic comeback. It was the kind of comeback a ten-year-old would make. On an off day. Mr. Wendt (a squirrelly, mean-spirited guy) had asked Noah which mid-twentieth-century fascist dictator was also known as "Il Duce." And Noah had replied: "You?"

And *that* had landed him here on Olsen's couch.

It was a shame, really. Noah had wasted any future opportunities to dazzle the other students with his wit. And he'd wasted it on nothing. A throwaway. Because Mr. Wendt had made it very clear that the next wisecrack, no matter how small, would get Noah kicked out of class. For good. Not that getting kicked out of that class would be any *huge* loss, but still. Noah was sort of interested in modern European history. . . .

"Well?" Olsen pressed.

Noah shrugged. "The usual, I guess." He sighed deeply. "It all started when I was a boy. My father is a proud man, and my upbringing was—"

"Noah!" Olsen raised his hands. "I don't want to hear it."

"Oh," Noah said. He bit his lip. "So does that mean I can go now?"

Olsen shook his head. "No. No, it doesn't. There's a matter I want to discuss with you. Your extracurriculars. Specifically, your total lack thereof."

Noah frowned. *This* was a surprise. He didn't know quite what to make of it. On one hand, he was shocked (rather pleasantly, in fact) that Olsen had even bothered to check on his extracurriculars. The man must have cared about him. A little bit, anyway. On the other hand, he felt bristly and defensive. Who was Olsen to criticize him for his lack of extracurriculars? These activities were so named for a reason: They were *outside* the curriculum. They were optional. And on the *other* hand . . . no, wait. That was three hands. . . .

"It just doesn't make any sense, Noah," Olsen said. "This is fall trimester, senior year. Crunch time. The time to impress colleges. I was just telling Sunday Winthrop, in fact, that . . ."

Sunday Winthrop. Thank God Olsen mentioned *her.* Because in that instant, a vision of Sunday—in one of those priceless long skirts, or maybe a bikini . . . yeah, a bikini—swept into Noah's brain and wiped it clear of any dangerous thoughts. . . .

And then she was gone.

Noah bowed his head. Wild, beer—commercial-like fantasies could only shut out the truth for so long. He had to face Olsen's words. He knew that colleges were watching him now. And that was precisely *why* he had bagged on all of his extracurriculars. He was sabotaging himself. The idea of filling out applications, of going on interviews, of touring strange campuses . . . it filled him with a profound dread. It *terrified* him.

He knew the source of the terror, too. It was quite

simple, really. He didn't want anything to change. After three arduous years, he'd finally reached an ideal comfort-zone—a sort of plateau where everything was wonderfully static. He did the same old things; he hung out with the same old crowd; he obsessed over the same old girl. The climb had nearly cost him his sanity. More than once. He'd played a lot of mind games, and suffered a lot of turmoil, and popped a lot of zits—and accidentally destroyed some valuable school property along the way.

But he'd *made* it. He'd hit a perfect standstill. And now they were asking him to give that up? No way. It wasn't fair. It wasn't *right*. In a perfect world, he would simply be allowed to flunk senior year and repeat it, again and again and again, to fall into an infinite cycle. . . .

"Noah!"

He glanced up. Olsen was glaring at him. His jowls were quivering.

"Yes?" Noah asked.

"Why aren't you listening to me?" he demanded.

"Uh . . . well, I—"

"Just look at your academic record." Olsen slapped a manila folder down on the desk. "You've dropped out of the Audio-Visual Club. You've dropped out of the French Literature Club. And what about Interscholastic Ultimate Frisbee?" Suddenly, Olsen's face grew almost pleading. "The Wessex Warriors need you. What with our basketball and lacrosse teams, we have the opportunity to take home *three* trophies this year. You're an integral part of that Frisbee unit. Everyone says so."

Noah leaned forward on the couch and peered at the file.

His eyes narrowed. There didn't seem to be anything in it. It was just an empty manila folder with his name on it.

"Um . . . can I take a look at this?" he asked.

Olsen snatched the folder back and shoved it into his drawer, slamming it shut with a clumsy thud. "No," he said.

"That's just a prop, right?"

"Excuse me?"

"A prop. You know, a theatrical device. It's used to heighten suspension of disbelief—"

"I know what a prop is, Noah. And, no, this isn't one of those. It's your record. It's *real*. Colleges will examine it."

Noah nodded. So. Olsen was calling his bluff. He was trying to intimidate him. With a piece of folded cardboard and a jowly poker face. Interesting move. And rare for Olsen.

"Oh," Noah said. "Sorry. See, it's just . . . ah, well, I guess props have been on my mind a lot lately. Because contrary to what you're suggesting here, I *am* involved in an extracurricular activity. A very important one, I might add."

Olsen stared at him over the rims of his glasses.

"I haven't told anyone this yet," Noah murmured, leaning forward. "So I tell you now in the strictest of confidence. I'm starting a guerrilla barbershop quartet."

"A what?"

"A guerrilla barbershop quartet. I'm gonna call it 'The Schwa Sound.' You know, after that little upside-down *E* that dictionaries use. Meaning the sound of neutrality. It'll be this sort of avant-garde, performance art troupe. It'll blur the line between theater and reality. It'll make a social and political statement. We're going to be strictly a cappella." Noah winked. "And strictly Metallica."

Olsen didn't respond.

Noah cleared his throat. "See, we're only going to do Metallica covers. But in the barbershop style. Old-timey, four-part harmony. And we're not going to announce any of our gigs. Instead, we'll carry our props and stage show with us wherever we go. We'll burst in on people." As Noah continued, he began gesturing wildly. His voice grew louder, too; it built in a frenzied crescendo that was deliberately reminiscent of the Beatles' song "A Day in the Life"—the part when all the instruments unite in cacophony at an increasingly higher pitch. "We'll have a backdrop that'll be very industrial, very jagged, almost post-apocalyptic. A lot of heavy machinery, power tools, torn buildings—but we're going to build it completely . . ."

And just as the Beatles did in "A Day in the Life" (when the mad swell of the music reached its boiling point and could go no further), Noah abruptly stopped, ending his monologue with the same kind of thunderous, single-chord finale:

" . . . out of Nerf."

Olsen blinked. "Nerf?"

"Nerf." Noah leaned back in the couch. "It's a kind of spongy material that they use to make toy footballs—"

"I know what Nerf is, Noah."

"Oh."

Olsen sighed. "What compels you to do this?"

"Well, I think that this kind of project—one that's outside the realm of school-sanctioned extracurriculars—demonstrates a certain creativity and initiative that colleges will appreciate—"

"I'm not talking about your *project,*" Olsen interrupted. "I'm asking what compels you to play these little charades for me. All the world's a stage, eh?"

Noah opened his mouth, then closed it. That comment was also extremely un-Olsen-like. Except for the Shakespeare part. It was penetrating. Insightful. It cut to the root of Noah's character, his very freakiness. And Noah knew how he *could* answer, at least in terms of *this* charade: He'd just been reacting to the academic record threat. He'd been hamming it up for hamming's sake. But maybe he shouldn't keep trying to BS his way out of this one. If Olsen wanted to get real, maybe *he* should, too.

"Because I'm scared," Noah said finally.

Olsen's face creased with concern. "Scared? Of what?"

"Of graduating," Noah mumbled.

"I don't understand," Olsen said. "You're scared of graduating, so you . . ." He left the sentence hanging.

"How should I know?" Noah shrugged. "I asked to be put in therapy, didn't I?"

Olsen smiled. "Okay. I think I get your drift. Noah, graduating is a *good* thing. You're growing up. Moving on. It's the first step toward adulthood." He leaned across the desk. "And, yes, fear is natural. But as the Bard says, 'Have patience and endure.'"

Noah stared down at his shoes. *Oh, boy.* When Olsen broke out with the Shakespeare twice in one minute, you knew it was time to leave. Sure, Noah wanted to open up a little. But he sure as hell didn't want this session to degenerate into some kind of wacked-out Elizabethan Hallmark moment.

"Maybe you need to experiment with a little change," Olsen said.

Noah's head shot up in alarm. "What do you mean?"

"Nothing major. Just . . . you know, try something you've never done before." Olsen leaned back in his chair and removed his spectacles, then fished a handkerchief out of his pocket and began wiping them. "Noah, I know I don't have to tell you that you're one of our brightest students. You consistently make Dean's list with very little effort. You're a lot like your dad in that way. But maybe it's time you start applying yourself in constructive ways."

Uh-oh. The word "constructive" always gave Noah the willies. He didn't even want to think about what Olsen had in mind. *The Dead Poets Society*? No, thanks.

But, then . . . maybe Olsen had a valid point.

Maybe Noah *should* start applying himself in more positive ways. He could volunteer to be a peer counselor or something . . . for freshmen. Brilliant! That would look great on a college application. He could help freshmen get in touch with their inner demons—the demons that convinced troubled young kids at boarding school to blow up toilets and invent a cappella groups like "The Schwa Sound." Right. It would be like being a shrink. Besides, shrinks were usually a little troubled themselves, right?

On the other hand, did he really want to devote any time to hanging out with freshmen?

No. Not really. After all, he remembered how messed-up *he* was as a freshman. That was a dark, dark time. It made his current mental state look perfectly stable. He didn't really want to go back there, not even as a tourist. So maybe he could help kids his own age. His own age or older. Like Fred, for instance. The guy was obviously pissed off about something. And it had nothing to do with his stolen La-Z-Boy. No, Fred Wright had been angry from the moment he'd arrived at Wessex. But Noah could help Fred to discover the roots of his anger, to manage it. And in doing so, he could also show Fred the *true* Wessex—the Wessex a PG would never see. He would bring Fred into the tight inner circle, Allison Scott be damned.

Okay, he would *try*, anyway. At the very least, it would be a fascinating social experiment (hey, like the time capsule!)—to become very good friends with somebody outside the circle of ABs. And it certainly qualified as a legitimate extracurricular activity . . . as far as Noah was concerned. And Fred would probably get a kick out of it. From what

Noah had seen so far, the guy was pretty cool. He was probably a lot cooler than Noah's "normal" friends, in fact.

"Well?" Olsen asked, putting his glasses back on. "What do you say?"

"I'll think about it," Noah answered with a smile.

"Don't think too long. As I said—"

"This is crunch time," Noah finished.

"Right." Olsen's face grew serious. "And, Noah? If you keep getting sent to my office, then you really *will* have to worry about graduating. Got it?"

"Got it," Noah said. "Thanks, Headmaster Olsen."

He jumped up and slung his knapsack over his shoulder, then burst out into the cold stone hall. He actually felt pretty decent. He could see himself really getting into playing this friend/mentor/shrink role with Fred. He would start right now, in fact. And hey, why stop there? He would also convince Sunday Winthrop to marry him. Then life would be just about perfect.

And *then* he'd be ready to graduate.

After classes ended, Noah still felt pretty optimistic— at least until he caught up with Fred. It was about six o'clock. The sun was a fiery red ball over the west side of campus. Fred was playing basketball on the cement court behind the dining hall. It was him versus another kid on the basketball team—that red-haired guy, Tony Viverito.

Well, they weren't *playing*, really. It was more like they were getting ready to play. A few people were watching them, too: Sunday and Winnie . . . and Tony's girlfriend—the Wiccan, the vampire with a day pass. What was her name? Sarah Mullins. Right.

For some reason, the atmosphere was very strained. Nobody spoke. Everybody seemed tense and jittery, as if a fight might break out. Except for Fred. He just stood at the half-court line, dribbling the ball and grinning at Tony.

Tony wasn't grinning back.

Noah walked up to Sunday and Winnie.

"Hey," he whispered. "What's going on?"

"Tony's forcing Fred to play a game with him," Sunday murmured. She stared at Fred. Her eyebrows were tightly knit. "Fred doesn't want to do it."

"Um . . . what?"

"I think he's worried about making Tony look bad," Sunday breathed.

Noah turned toward the court.

"What are you scared of, dude?" Tony suddenly demanded. He stepped forward and snatched the ball from Fred's grasp. "You scared that people will see that you suck?"

Fred chuckled. "Look, Tony, I just want to shoot around."

"You're a freakin' chump," Tony snapped. "You know that?"

Whoa. Major tension. Noah glanced at Sunday. She was chewing her lip. If he didn't know any better, he might actually think that Sunday was *concerned* about Fred—at least, judging from the look in those dark eyes. But how was that possible? She didn't know Fred. And if she actually wanted to know Fred, she would have to go through Noah, because from now on, Noah would be facilitating all interaction between Fred and the ABs. . . .

"Well, this is much too exciting for me," Winnie said. "I'll see you later." He paused. "Oh, by the way, the school store is out of notebooks. But I got a couple of extra ones, if you guys want to buy some from me."

Noah rolled his eyes, momentarily forgetting the odd showdown on the court. "Jesus, Winnie. You bought out all the notebooks?"

Winnie shrugged. "Did I say that?" He headed toward the dining hall.

"Great, man," Noah called after him. "Thanks a lot. You know, maybe I just won't take notes this year. Maybe I'll just use my photographic memory. . . ." His voice trailed off.

He laughed. He should have seen it coming. At the beginning of every year, Winnie cleaned out at least one item from the school store. Entirely. As if monopolizing the tobacco market wasn't enough. Last year it had been cassettes. The year before that, batteries. He simply waltzed in and signed for the merchandise on his student account number. The charges were then billed to his parents. Some parents would be puzzled to receive a bill for a thousand dollars worth of batteries. Some might even be pissed. Noah's own dad would certainly fall into the latter category; he deducted every school store charge from Noah's allowance. But Winnie's father never saw the school store bills. That was the beauty of the scam. Mr. Ellis had his personal accountant take care of all of Winnie's expenses, no questions asked. So Winnie could sign for as much as he wanted, then charge all the students cash to buy stuff from *him*. It was free money in his pocket.

"Uh-oh," Sunday murmured.

Noah glanced back at the game.

Without warning, Fred lunged forward and swatted the ball out of Tony's hands, simultaneously lowering his left shoulder into Tony's chest. Tony staggered backward. *Ow.* Noah cringed. That definitely hurt. But Fred didn't stop. In one fluid motion, he scooped the ball off the bounce and dribbled full-speed toward the basket. His expression was one of absolute calm. The moment he crossed the free-throw line, he leaped gracefully off one foot and rotated 360 degrees, like a ballet dancer. Noah's jaw dropped. As Fred completed the spin, he lifted the ball with one hand and flicked it into the air with a delicate roll off his fingers. It sailed up in a high arc, then plopped through the net. *Swish.*

"Jesus," Noah muttered.

Fred landed on both feet. He caught the ball before it hit the ground. "What's that about being a chump?" he asked, turning to Tony.

Tony rubbed his chest and glared at him. "That wouldn't have counted in a game," he spat. "You charged me."

Noah stole a quick peek at Sunday. She was shaking her head. But he couldn't tell if it was a disapproving shake at the dirty move, or a shake of awe at Fred's prodigious talent. He sort of hoped it was the former.

"It would have counted where I come from," Fred stated dryly. "Look, man, I told you, I don't want any trouble. We're teammates. I just want to shoot around with you—"

"Oh, they play dirty in D.C.?" Tony interrupted. He took a step toward Fred.

"Okay, Tony, just chill out," Sarah Mullins groaned. She hurried onto the court, her black dress billowing behind her. She wrapped her arm around Tony's shoulder and gently guided him in the opposite direction. "If you don't want to shoot around, let's just get out of here."

Tony scowled at Fred as he shambled off the court. "The coach is gonna love having a cheater on his team," he snarled. "Just wait and see."

Fred sighed. "Look, I'm sorry if I bumped you, all right? It's just, you were kind of egging me on, you know? Besides, your feet weren't planted, so it wasn't really a charge. And I just wanted to . . ." He didn't finish.

Sarah and Tony disappeared behind the dining hall.

"How did this all start?" Noah asked Sunday, baffled.

"I'm not really sure." She walked out onto the court. Noah trotted after her.

Fred grinned ruefully at the two of them. "I probably shouldn't have done that," he said.

"Done what?" Sunday asked. "Schooled Tony Viverito? Of course you should have."

Schooled? Noah stared at her. In thirteen years of hanging out with Sunday, he had never once heard her use the term "schooled." In fact, now that he thought about it, everything about the way she was carrying herself right now seemed just a little . . . *different.* Her hands were in her pockets, and she was sort of listing to one side. It was a laid-back pose.

Too laid back. Almost as if she were trying to mimic Fred. Well, either that or impress him.

"Maybe I should try to catch up with him," Fred said.

Sunday shook her head. "He'll get over it."

Fred nodded. "Hey—I was thinking about what you said earlier. You know, about the student council. And I don't know if I'm willing to accept it."

She was smiling now, too. "Accept what?"

"That I can't run for it." He started dribbling the ball, but his eyes remained glued to Sunday. "I mean, shouldn't there be some non-ABs on it? You know, somebody to represent the interest of the common folk, like me and Sarah and Tony?"

Sunday laughed. "Yeah, there should, but it won't happen."

"Well, can't I just come to the dinner with you?" Fred asked. "You know, as your guest or something?"

"I don't think so," she said, lowering her gaze. Her face seemed flushed.

"Well, how about if I bring a dish?" Fred prompted.

Sunday laughed again. "No need. Burwell supplies all the food and drink."

"Really?" Fred stopped bouncing the ball. "I didn't know he was a chef."

"He gets it catered," Sunday said. "Except for the punch. He makes a mean punch."

Fred nodded slowly. "Punch, huh? Interesting. Very interesting . . ."

Noah's eyes kept flashing back and forth between the two of them. They were inching closer and closer to each other. It was as if their noses were connected by an invisible fishing line. It suddenly became very clear to him what was going on here. Sure. He'd been to enough of his parents' cocktail parties to spot this particular brand of silly back-and-forth. It was called "flirting." He was no good at it himself, of course.

"Why do you want to be on the student council so badly, anyway?" Sunday asked.

Fred shrugged. "Like I told you. To take the BS out of Boarding School."

Both of them started cracking up.

Noah pursed his lips. That was the lamest joke he'd ever heard. *He* was the top-notch comedian here, not Fred. Didn't Sunday know that? Okay, that clinched it. It was a good thing he'd vowed to become Fred's personal mentor/shrink/etcetera. Noah would *definitely* have to keep an eye on him. Yup, from now on, Noah wasn't going to let Fred Wright out of his sight. Not for a second.

Note to Sunday from Allison

Hadley Bryant told me that she saw you making out with that guy Fred What's-his-name. Now of course I don't believe her, but as we all know, every rumor is founded in some truth.

Sunday's reply to Allison

Actually, we had sex in a hundred different positions, including the wheelbarrow.

Note to Sunday from Mackenzie

Hi, sweetie! Hadley Bryant told me that she saw you hooking up with that new guy in the woods. He's so hot! I'm jealous. My horoscope says to play things cool in the romance department. Why? Why can't I find love?

Sunday's reply to Mackenzie

Not all of us can be so lucky, Mack. Listen to your horoscope. Patience, dear. Patience.

Part III:
"Dude!"

Fred Wright's Letter to Jim Simmons

Hey man,

I bet you never thought I was much of a letter-writer, huh? Well, that just goes to show you how much boarding school has changed me. In two short weeks, I've already become a man of arts and letters.

Wait, did I say arts and letters? I meant farts and letters.

HA!!!

Sorry. That was painful. I just had to hit you with a little old-school Lincoln locker-room humor. My brain has been working overtime. It needs to be stupid right now. I actually had classes today. They have classes on Saturday here. Can you believe that crap?

So, how's college life treating you? Are the chicks out in California as hot as everybody says they are? I hope so. I hope they aren't as totally wack as they are here. James, my friend, you would not believe this place. Saturday classes are just the tip of the iceberg. Even the girls' names are off the hook. Everybody has a last name for a first name and vice versa. They're all named Campbell or Mackenzie or Spencer or Hadley. Guys, too. I'm not joking. It's nuts.

I have met this one sort of cool girl, though. Sunday Winthrop. She's part of this clique called "Alumni Brats." It would take too long to explain. Let's just say that she owns about twelve pairs of shoes, and each pair costs more than

Diane's entire wardrobe put together. And I dig that. Diane always tried to pretend like she wasn't rich. But Sunday really gets off on it.

She's also in my math class. It's taught by my dorm adviser, a guy named Burwell who I'm certain is wanted in several states for murder. The fat bastard stole my La-Z-Boy.

So, no, Jim. In answer to your question, boarding school isn't exactly what I expected.

Luckily, this guy Noah has been showing me the ropes. Well, either that or he's in love with me. He won't leave me alone. You should meet him some time. Soon, though. I'm pretty sure he'll be locked away in an asylum before the year's out. He dresses up for class every day in a blazer and khakis. He never shuts up, either. But he's got a killer CD collection. He must have five hundred CDs in his room. He has every single Beatles, Zeppelin, and Hendrix outtake, bootleg, or previously unreleased . . .

Oh! That's right. I forgot. You like sissy white-boy alt-rock. Which reminds me, there's also a kid here named Hobson who looks like a sissy white boy but fancies himself the next Snoop Doggy Dogg. Oh, yeah, and there's a chubby guy named Winnie, who was indicted for fraud by the Securities Exchange Commission last year. He's my dip dealer. If I try to buy my own dip, he'll rat me out and get me suspended. He runs a monopoly on all illegal substances—booze, smokes, probably drugs, too. And school supplies.

Jim! Help me! Take me home! Get me out of this place! Ahhh!

sorry. Just had to freak out there for a second. It's really not that bad. I actually have a few goals now. In no particular order, they are as follows:

1) Get Burwell back for stealing my chair.

2) Prove to everybody around here that Winnie isn't the only guy who can get his hands on contraband.

3) Get elected to the student council. And if I can't do that, make sure the student council meetings turn into orgies of peace and free love.

The amazing thing is, I think I will accomplish all three of these goals tonight. Or two and a half, anyway.

All right, I admit it. That's actually the REAL reason I'm writing you. I just have to brag right now. You see, James, my friend, I just returned from pulling a very, very sweet prank. I skipped my last class and ditched Noah long enough to score two big plastic bottles of vodka at the one liquor store in town. It was really easy. Those expensive fake IDs we got this summer work wonders in rural Connecticut. Booze up here is cheap, too. Twenty-five bucks total.

I didn't get it for personal consumption, though. I used it to spike Mr. Burwell's student council dinner punch. He was stupid enough to leave the jugs of it sitting right out in our headmaster's backyard. Anyone could have messed with it. All I had to do was hop the fence and pour the stuff in. It took less than a minute. It was freaking beautiful, man. I was like some kind of commando, following Burwell around with this knapsack full of bottles, waiting for the opportune moment to strike.

All right, maybe you had to be there to appreciate it.

Anyway, this is what my life has come to, Jim. Petty revenge. It's sad, but at least it keeps me off the street. I'll let you know if I get caught.

> Your pal,
> Fred

P.S. Don't start smoking weed, all right? I hear they smoke a lot of weed in California.

P.P.S. If you don't write back, I won't be offended. I'll just assume you actually have real new friends and a normal life. Unlike some of us.

P.P.P.S. You would be very proud of me. I've finally thrown out Salvatore's letter. And I'm down to fantasizing about brutally murdering Diane only five times a day. Tops.

Interoffice memorandum

To: PO
From: PB
Date: 9/30
Re: Fred Wright

I don't like this buddy-buddy relationship he has going with NP. They're much too freindly right now. I hear them down in NP's room at all hours, listening to loud rock music. NP says they're starting a gorilla barbershop group. I don't like the sound of that. Might interfere with strategic maneuvers. My plan of action would be to put surveillance on him, maybe scare him a little. Kid's enough of a wise-ass as it is. He needs discipline. What do you think?

- - - - - - - - - - -

Interoffice memorandum

To: PB
From: PO
Date: 9/30
Re: No subject

Just a reminder: I make the suggestions. And in the future, don't ever discuss such matters via interoffice memorandum again. Understood? Incidentally, your spelling is atrocious.

10

"Psst. Sunday. Does this punch taste funny to you?"

Sunday glanced up at Noah. For some reason, the question struck her as very silly. So did the way he was standing. He was leaning close to her, whispering—but he was also draped over Olsen's antique globe, as if the only thing that could possibly keep him from falling over was a scale model of Planet Earth, circa 1768. And his tie was very loose. His wavy, brown hair was a mess. One cowlick stuck out from behind his right ear.

She giggled.

"That's what I thought," Noah muttered. He stumbled out of Olsen's living room and disappeared around the corner, through the front hall.

"What did he just say?" Mackenzie asked.

"He asked if the punch tasted funny," Sunday replied. She tried to frown, but she couldn't stop grinning. What was her problem? She peered into the plastic cup in her hand. It didn't look any different. Nope. Just the dregs of plain old red fruit punch. The same kind of punch Mr. Burwell brought to *every* student council dinner. Glorified bug juice. But now that she thought about it, there was a sort of odd tang. . . .

"Sure, it tastes funny," Mackenzie whispered. "Somebody spiked it."

Sunday's head snapped up. Then she burst out laughing.

"Shh," Mackenzie whispered. But she laughed, too. She glanced around Olsen's living room. But nobody was there. Everybody was in Olsen's den, huddled around the punch bowl.

"Are you *serious*?" Sunday breathed.

"Well, yeah," Mackenzie said, without the least bit of surprise. "Can't you taste it? There's really cheap vodka in it. But I just assumed that Noah was the one who put it in there. It seems like a Noah kind of thing to do, doesn't it?"

Sunday blinked. Wow. She was having a hard time focusing. Mackenzie's big brown eyes suddenly seemed wider than ever, like two pools of cocoa. Another smile crept across Sunday's face. She was actually pretty tipsy, now that she thought about it. *Cool.* But she felt oddly detached from the situation. And the detachment was nice. Very nice. No wonder Olsen's mansion seemed particularly inviting and cozy tonight. No wonder her dress seemed extra-comfortable. For once, she was actually *psyched* for a student council meeting.

"Maybe Noah *was* the one who spiked it," Sunday whispered. "I mean, wouldn't it also be a Noah kind of thing to spike the punch, then go around and ask everyone if it tasted funny?"

Mackenzie shook her head. "I don't know. . . ."

"So who do you think did it?"

"Winnie. I bet it was Winnie." Mackenzie took another big gulp.

Sunday thought for a second. "Winnie? Nah. He's too much of an ass-kisser. He'd never do something that could get him in trouble with Olsen directly. That's not his style. He's all about being sneaky and ripping people off. Maybe it was Burwell himself."

"No . . . he wouldn't want to get kids drunk. He's always quoting the orientation handbook. I bet this has something to do with the plot." Mackenzie drained her glass and fixed Sunday with a somber gaze. "You know, the conspiracy."

Sunday started giggling again.

"Why do you always *do* that?" Mackenzie asked. She tried to frown, but she ended up giggling, too. "How come you don't believe me?"

"I'm sorry, I'm sorry." Sunday finished her own glass. "It's just, I don't know. I mean, sure I could believe in a conspiracy. Just not with those three people. Winnie's too selfish to be on a plot with anyone else, and Olsen's too much of a . . . well, a buffoon." She bit her lip, wondering if she sounded too harsh. She didn't want to hurt Mackenzie's feelings. "I don't know. Do you have any proof?"

Mackenzie sighed, making a pouty face. "Well, no. Nothing concrete. But I've seen some weird stuff. Like, I saw this note in Winnie's notebook. . . ." Her voice trailed off. She smiled again. "Okay. Maybe you're right. Maybe it sounds crazy. But as soon as I get something concrete, I'll show it to you. How's that?"

Sunday nodded. "Cool." She glanced down at their cups. "How about a refill?"

"Definitely." Mackenzie sighed. Her eyes glazed over. "You know, I still can't get over how Miss Burke is here. Isn't that just the best?" She leaned close to Sunday as they made their way through the house toward the den. "Miss Burke is gonna totally turn the student council around," she whispered in a faraway voice. "We need a young faculty adviser, you know? Somebody besides Mr. Burwell. Some new blood. This year is gonna rule."

Hmm. If Sunday didn't know better, she might think that Mackenzie had developed a new crush. But Mackenzie had promised Sunday that she'd sworn off crushes—several years ago, right after the lead singer of No Doubt started going out with the lead singer of Bush. Mackenzie had been devastated by that. She had vowed she would never fall for another older woman again. Then again, this *was* Mackenzie. She had also once vowed that she would never mention the number twenty-seven in Sunday's presence again, either.

"And you know what else? I found out Miss Burke was born on April twenty-seventh. So she's a Taurus—a Scorpio's ideal match. *Plus* she has the number twenty-seven in her birthday."

Yup. Sunday smiled to herself. Major crush.

And judging from the scene in the den, Mackenzie wasn't the only one. *Good Lord.* Sunday couldn't believe it. Miss Burke was *the* life of the party. She was standing right next to the punch bowl, surrounded by Winnie, Noah, and Hobson. All three stood in a tight huddle around her, clutching their cups—looking very much like the schoolboys they were. In fact, their jackets and ties somehow made them look even *younger* . . . in a cute way, though. (Well, except for Hobson, who was gangsta'd up in a full-fledged, white seersucker suit.) All three were grinning stupidly. Pretty much panting, in fact.

Sunday couldn't really blame them, of course. No. She knew how testosterone worked in conjunction with booze. And that dress Miss Burke was wearing . . . whew. It was a short, black, spaghetti-strap deal (a Vera Wang, maybe?)—the kind of dress a girl would wear for a night out in New York or Paris or Milan. Not the kind of dress that made a lot of appearances at Olsen's student council dinners. Especially not on a teacher.

Sunday glanced at Mackenzie.

Mackenzie swerved slightly. She seemed unsure of herself.

"Let's get that drink, huh?" Sunday suggested. She pulled Mackenzie toward the circle.

" . . . and that's why I think *all* of you should apply to Wesleyan," Miss Burke was saying. She smiled coyly. "You'd feel right at home there after Wessex."

The boys burst out laughing, as if that were the funniest thing anyone had ever said.

Sunday tried not to roll her eyes. It wasn't so much that the boys were making asses of themselves.

She could handle that. It was more that the topic of conversation was college applications. *Again?* Couldn't anyone talk about anything else? She took Mackenzie's cup and ladled in a healthy serving of punch from the crystal bowl on the buffet table, then did the same for herself. She suddenly wished Fred were here. A fleeting smile crossed her face. *He* wouldn't talk about college applications. He'd probably ask them all to do trust falls. . . .

After taking the cup from Sunday, Mackenzie cleared her throat, then forced herself into the huddle—right between Noah and Winnie.

"Hey, Noah?" she asked, even though she was staring at Miss Burke with a big, drunken smile. "Can I ask you a question?"

Noah grinned. "Um . . . sure. I'm over here, though."

Mackenzie didn't seem to hear him. "See, it's been bothering me since that first day of class. How did you know what postmodernism was? I mean, how did you know what Miss Burke was talking about?"

"Because at the time, I was making a self-referential joke," Noah said. "Postmodernism is self-referential."

Sunday began to notice something odd. Besides the conversation, that is. Miss Burke was gazing at

Noah. Actually, she was giving Noah the same kind of adoring, undivided attention that Mackenzie was giving *her*.

Sunday's eyes narrowed. Was she just imagining things? The punch was pretty strong. But, no . . . there was a difference between listening to someone and *listening* to someone. She'd been to enough of her parents' cocktail parties to know the difference when she saw it. Or so she thought. Flirting with Noah, though? Not only was it unethical (and criminal)—it was just plain weird. Maybe Miss Burke was having a bad reaction to the alcohol.

"Why don't you explain what you mean, Noah," Miss Burke murmured.

"Yeah, homeboy," Hobson chimed in. "Kick it."

"Well . . . I mean, I don't know," Noah said. He shrugged. "Pretty much *everything* today is self-referential. That's why I live my life the way I do."

Miss Burke laughed.

Mackenzie seemed confused. So did Hobson. So did Winnie. Sunday felt pretty confused herself.

Noah turned to Miss Burke. "I mean, just look at all the movies and sitcoms coming out. Pretty much every one of them has a role for an actor who plays *that* actor. You know, 'This week, Charlie Sheen guest-stars as himself.' It's this weird cult of celebrity. My theory is, pretty soon, there won't be any more actors playing roles. They'll just all be playing themselves. You know, all the marquees will be like: 'Gwyneth Paltrow *as* Gwyneth Paltrow.'"

"I could easily see that," Miss Burke breathed. She leaned forward and draped a hand over Noah's shoulder. "Easily."

Okay. Sunday took a sip of punch. She was *definitely* not imagining things. This had gone beyond flirtatious. This was downright steamy. . . .

A bunch of spindly fingers seized Sunday's arm. *Ouch.*

She glanced up to find Allison's teeth grinding in her face.

"Hey," Sunday said. "You're hurting—"

"Come with me," Allison grunted. She jerked Sunday away from the circle. A couple of drops of Sunday's punch spilled onto the floor. "Headmaster Olsen and Mr. Burwell need some help setting the table."

"But wait a sec," Sunday protested. She glanced over her shoulder as Allison dragged her into the dining room. Miss Burke's arm was still draped over Noah. "I just want to—"

"Can you *believe* that woman?" Allison hissed. She came to an abrupt halt next to Olsen's medieval-style banquet table. "I've got to find Olsen right now. Have you seen him?"

"I thought you said he needed help setting . . ." Sunday didn't finish. She frowned at all the silver and crystal and perfectly folded napkins. The table was done. It was *more* than done. It was fit for a museum. She turned to Allison. "What's going on?"

"I just needed an excuse to get you out of there," Allison mumbled. She started pacing back and forth. "I just can't believe this kind of thing is going on under Olsen's roof. I mean, it's just—I mean, *can you*?" she sputtered.

Sunday sighed. "You know what, Al? Maybe you should have some punch. I bet that would make you feel a lot better."

Allison stopped pacing. She glared at Sunday. "Why would *punch* make me feel better?"

"Well, have you had any yet?" Sunday asked. She wriggled her eyebrows suggestively.

"Two glasses," Allison said.

Sunday blinked. "And you don't feel better?"

"No. What are you talking about? Why should I feel *better*?" She started pacing again. "If you want to know the truth, it's making me a little queasy. It tastes funny. Burwell must have switched brands this year."

Switched brands. Sunday giggled, but quickly stopped herself. She took another long sip from her own cup. Well. That was certainly an interesting interpretation. Very creative, actually. Sunday didn't know if she would have been able to come up with that one herself.

"What's so funny?" Allison asked.

Sunday glanced around to make sure nobody could hear them, then stepped closer.

"Somebody spiked the punch," she whispered. "You haven't noticed?"

Allison rolled her eyes. "Please, Sunday. I'm not in the mood."

"What? I'm *serious.* There's vodka in—"

"Can we please stop talking about the *punch?*" Allison interrupted.

Sunday hesitated. But she saw that there was no point in continuing. Why try to convince Allison that the punch had been spiked? She simply wouldn't accept it. She'd made up her mind. It was just another addition to the great big list of Allison Scott's Denials. Like Hobson's breakup. Like Sunday's desire to decorate her own bedroom. If Allison wanted to believe something, she *believed* it. Everybody else could go to hell.

Funny. She was a lot like Sunday's parents that way.

All of a sudden, Sunday realized she was pissed off. And why? This should be *fun.* But being around Allison just made her feel as if she were being smothered with a heavy, fluffy, very expensive pillow. She couldn't *breathe*—much less make herself heard. Allison's denial ensured that she always got what she wanted. Always.

Hiring that interior decorator for their suite was a perfect example. *"I made an investment in Sven Larsen,"* Allison had told her. *"Someday, you'll come to appreciate that. Maybe not now, but eventually."* So Sunday had given in. To a whole year of "stark absences." It killed her, but she did it. In those situations, it was best not to fight. Fighting only brought more misery. Some battles just couldn't be won. She just wished she lived in a single.

Like Fred.

Her anger began to fade. She sighed and stared into her cup, deliriously confused. Why was it that every train of thought kept leading her back to Fred? The guy wasn't *right* for her. Instinctively, she knew that. But she couldn't stop picturing the way he'd loped across that basketball court and whirled in the air. . . .

"I just don't get it," Allison muttered, circling the long table. "Here's this woman who clearly has a lot of issues, and she's a *teacher*. I mean, she just has no place at this school. And the way she's acting with Hobson and the rest of them! Can you believe that? Actually, what I can't believe is that *they're* allowing it to happen. Hobson should know better—"

"Oh, come on, Al," Sunday gently interrupted. "Let 'em have their fun. It's every Wessex boy's dream to scam on a hot new teacher."

Allison froze. *"What?"* she cried, aghast.

Sunday shrugged, then finished the rest of her cup. "Forget it," she mumbled. "You know what everybody at this school neez . . . I mean needs?" *Uh-oh.* She was starting to slur her speech. "A big, fat dose of Fred Wright."

Allison just gaped at her.

Whatever. Sunday headed back for punch number three.

From the Desk of Principal Morris Otto

The Lincoln School
4500 Wisconsin Avenue
Washington, D.C. 20037

September 6
Mr. Phillip Olsen
The Wessex Academy
325 South Chapel Street
New Farmington, Connecticut 06744

Dear Mr. Olsen,

I am writing in regard to a former student
of mine, Frederick Wright. As I'm sure you
know, having read Mr. Wright's transcripts,
he has the potential to be an excellent
student. Unfortunately, as you also might
have guessed, he makes poor decisions.

My chief concern about Mr. Wright,
however, is a certain moral vacuum that I
have yet to encounter in other kids of his
ilk. As the principal of a public school,
I've had my share of experience with
juvenile delinquents. I've witnessed
troublemaking and reckless behavior of all
kinds. I could tell stories that would shock

a man like you — a man who has spent his career at a prestigious boarding school. We may not have your resources, Mr. Olsen, but we have heart, and we have good intentions. To put it bluntly, Mr. Wright went out of his way to thwart these good intentions. So consider this a friendly warning: This boy is bad news.

I'm sure you can appreciate my candor. And good luck with the basketball team!

Sincerely,
Principal Morris Otto

11

Dirty dancing. They were *dirty dancing*! In Olsen's living room.

It was . . .

Allison could think of only one word. Sickening.

She stood under the arch that divided the living room from the front hall, slowly crumpling her plastic cup in her hand. Enough was enough. What about dinner? They hadn't even *eaten* yet—well, except for some crummy hors d'oeuvres—and it was already pushing nine o'clock. She was hungry, dammit. This was a student council meeting. They had an *agenda*. And the sight of Mackenzie and Sunday, gyrating back-to-back—with those slinky smiles and their eyes closed and their hands up and their butts touching . . .

But that wasn't the worst of it. Oh, no. That wasn't the most egregious crime being committed in this room. An X-rated lesbian encounter between her two best friends was *far* preferable to what was going on with Hobson, Miss Burke, and the rest of the boys.

Miss Burke was teaching them how to do "The Hustle."

A teacher at the Wessex Academy was doing this. A member of the *faculty*.

"Dude!" they kept yelling. "Dude!"

And they were sticking their arms out and shaking their behinds . . . and it was just so disgraceful on so many levels—not the least of which was that The Hustle was certainly not a valid dance, even though Miss Burke claimed to be some kind of dance instructor; and they weren't even listening to the actual song . . . and what *was* this music, anyway? It was some *other* seventies disco crap about getting down and "making a little love." Or something. It certainly didn't sound like the kind of CD Olsen would have lying around his house.

Speaking of which, where *was* Olsen? And Mr. Burwell?

Allison tossed her balled-up cup into a wastebasket. Time to find them. They had barely made an appearance all night. Time to alert Olsen to the horrors unfolding in his very own home. Time to give him her list of grievances against Miss Burke.

Or maybe not. Maybe she should wait. Because now, of course, that list was far too long. A mere list wouldn't even suffice. No, sir.

She whirled and strode toward the staircase. She couldn't stand looking at Hobson for another second. Didn't he realize how badly he was embarrassing himself? It was beyond shameful. It was despicable. What would his father say? The hip-hop lingo was one thing. It was irritating, but it was just a fad. A phase. Hobson would get over it, just as he'd gotten over wearing his little sailor's suit as a boy. But to behave in *this* way, to dance around like a complete imbecile . . . it pointed at something deeper. More troubling. As if he were deliberately going out of his way to tarnish the Crowe name.

One thing was certain, though. The punch *was* spiked. Yes. Allison understood that now. She nodded to herself as she pounded up the stairwell, clutching her skirt to make sure she didn't trample on it. Somebody in that room down there must have been responsible. But nobody was talking. Even worse, nobody seemed to share her outrage. It was probably part of some big conspiracy to thwart the effectiveness of the student council. Maybe Mackenzie was right about that secret plot she kept talking about.

For all Allison knew, Hobson was the ringleader. . . .

What had happened to him, anyway? She paused at the top of the steps and bowed her head. The music drifted up from the first floor. She wanted to smash the stereo to pieces.

Hobson, Hobson, Hobson. He used to be so *sweet.* So normal. And there was still that sweetness deep inside him . . . but where?

No matter. She thrust her chin up. She would not wallow in self-pity. Everything would work out. He just needed time. He needed time to find himself again. The breakup was only temporary. Of course it was. She marched down the hall and knocked on Olsen's bedroom door.

"Headmaster Olsen?" she called. "Are you in there? It's Allison."

"Allison? Sorry. Just a minute. We'll be right out."

She frowned. Was Mr. Burwell in there, too? She leaned close, pressing her ear to the wood.

" . . . no problem," Olsen was muttering in a hushed voice. "The timing is great, but . . ."

Allison strained her ears, but lost him. It was tough to make anything out over the faint hum of the music. Something about . . . *"Georgetown."* The school? Probably.

There was a pause in his conversation.

Aha: He was talking on the phone.

Maybe somebody's parents wanted him to write a recommendation. Winnie was applying to Georgetown, wasn't he? She cupped her hands around her ear.

" . . . this is going to be the one. The one that'll put us over the top."

It was peculiar, though . . . the *way* Olsen was talking. Even though she could barely hear him, he sounded a little different. Maybe it was just her imagination. She *had* downed two cups of punch earlier in the evening. But no, she could tell that he wasn't speaking in his usual, plodding, formal, overly friendly way. He sounded more confident. In control. His tone was more casual, too. She smiled. This was an intriguing surprise. She'd always assumed that Olsen was too much of a simpleton to use different phone personas for different people.

" . . . yes, Georgetown is lovely at Christmastime." He laughed. "You ever been there? The diving is spectacular. I've become quite a scuba man. John Grisham was right."

Allison frowned. *John Grisham?* Olsen hated writers like John Grisham. He was strictly Shakespeare, all the way. And who went diving at Christmas in Georgetown?

"Listen, I'd better go. Paul and I have students waiting. Bye."

There was a click.

Whoops. Allison lurched away from the door. She plastered a smile on her face.

Mr. Burwell marched out first. He brushed past her and headed toward the stairs, grunting a "hello." Tonight's double-breasted suit was navy blue with white pinstripes.

Mr. Olsen followed behind him, hesitating in the doorway.

"Uh . . . hi, Headmaster Olsen," she said.

He peered at her over the rims of his spectacles. She swallowed. Could he tell she'd been eavesdropping?

Then he grinned. "Hi, Allison." He shook his head apologetically. "Sorry we've been holed up here for so long. Just had to make a few calls."

She nodded. "Of course. I just . . . um, I thought you should know—"

"I'm glad you came to find me," he said. "There's something . . ." He paused. "Sorry for interrupting. Do speak."

"No, no. Go ahead."

He sighed. "Well, there's a matter I wanted to discuss with you." He stepped aside and gestured for her to come in. "Please."

Allison hesitated. Her pulse picked up a notch. She had a terrible fear that he was going to reprimand her for using his bedroom to talk to Hobson during the Opening Day party. But no, he would have done that a while ago; besides, his expression was more grave than angry. So what was this about? Extracurriculars? She knew he'd been talking to every AB, one by one. But *her* record was stellar. . . .

"Have a seat," he said, closing the door behind them. He motioned her toward his desk chair and sat on the edge of his bed. "I want to talk to you about Sunday."

"Sunday?" *Interesting. Very interesting.* She sank into the chair. "What about her?"

Olsen chewed his lip. He flashed a strained smile. "This is always difficult for me. I hate to interfere in your lives." He slipped back into his old, familiar tone of voice. "But I just got off the phone with Sunday's parents. And, well . . . well, they're not particularly happy with the way this year is shaping up for her so far."

Allison nodded. No surprise there. *She* wasn't happy with the way Sunday's year was shaping up, either. Especially with her bitchiness about Sven Larsen's interior design. A lot of people would sell their souls just to get a *consultation* with that man.

"They're particularly concerned about her relationship with Fred Wright," Olsen said.

"Relationship?" Allison whispered.

Olsen nodded. "Yes."

My God. Allison knew that Sunday was inordinately obsessed with the guy—but for God's sake, she'd had no idea that there was any *relationship.* That joke about the wheelbarrow position . . . Allison's stomach turned. Oh, no. No way. That was definitely a joke. Wasn't it? Sunday hadn't sunk *that* low. She barely even *saw* Fred. They had one class together. The only one who seemed to have a relationship with Fred was Noah. Not that Allison could explain *that,* either. But at least Noah was a weirdo himself.

"Look, I don't know how far it's progressed," Olsen said. He removed his spectacles and wiped them with a handkerchief. "But Mr. Burwell informed me that they were passing notes in class. And the two of them were spotted walking into the woods together, behind the Arts Center. While Sunday was supposed to be in Art History, I might add."

"I . . . I had no idea," Allison breathed. She started shaking her head. This was terrible. Absolutely terrible. But the more she thought about it, the more it made sense. What about Sunday's little comment earlier this evening? *"You know what everybody at this school needs? A big, fat dose of Fred Wright."* And she was probably getting exactly that. Allison shuddered. It was . . . well, it was too awful to think about. What was happening to Sunday? What was happening to *everybody* at this school? They were all becoming degenerates. Just look at the scene in the living room. Booze and disco and lesbian butt-rubbing. It was a seventies-style Sodom and Gomorrah down there. A bacchanal of cheap smut. At a student council dinner . . .

"So I'm just going to be frank with you," Olsen said.

Allison nodded. She was starting to feel ill.

"I'd like you to talk to Sunday," he said. "Not on my behalf, nor on her parents behalf. Not even on *your* behalf. But on her behalf. For her own good." Olsen put his glasses back on and smiled apprecia-tively. "Listen, Allison. Deep down, Sunday knows better than to get too involved with somebody like Fred." He raised his hands. "Not to disparage him in any way. The boy has a lot of potential, a lot of talent and intelligence. . . ."

"Of course," Allison agreed. "Of course."

Olsen folded his hands in his lap. "I knew you'd understand. You of all people know that I wouldn't have accepted a postgraduate who wasn't up to the Wessex standard. It's just that Fred Wright . . . well, he has some maturing to do." Olsen titled his head. "And this is a critical time in Sunday's academic career. She can't afford to be distracted by someone who might not have her best interests at heart."

Allison nodded again. "I agree completely," she

said. "Don't worry, Headmaster Olsen. I'll talk to her."

She drew in her breath. The queasiness began to subside. Yes, she *would* talk to Sunday. After all, Sunday was one of her best friends. And Allison had sworn that she would devote herself this year to bonding, to reaffirming relationships. *Real* relationships. Ones forged by generations of family history. It was time for somebody to do something right for a change.

"Thank you," Olsen murmured. "And I know that I don't even have to mention that this is just between us."

"Of course not."

He smiled, then stood. "So what do you say we eat? I assume that's why you came to get me, right?" He chuckled. "'Come, come, Antipholus, we dine too late.'"

"Well, actually . . . um, I wanted to warn you."

His smile vanished. "Warn me?"

She nodded, easing out of her chair. "Well, I don't want to alarm you or anything. But somebody put alcohol in the punch. And everybody . . . well, they're a little drunk. They're actually dancing." She pointed at the floor, which was still vibrating with the distant sound of a monotonous disco beat. "Maybe you should just see for yourself."

Olsen just laughed again. "Oh, don't worry,

Allison. Nobody put any alcohol in the punch. I'm sure people are just joking around. They're using it as an excuse to dance while I'm upstairs." He pointed to an empty cup on his nightstand. "That's just plain old fruit punch. The same brand Mr. Burwell always provides. I've had several glasses myself."

Allison stared at him, shocked. "Are you *sure*?"

"Yes. I'm sure." He walked to the door and opened it, then turned to her. "Shall we?"

She searched his eyes.

And then it hit her: He was lying. He knew very well that the punch had been spiked. But he was deliberately denying it. Because if he denied it . . . well, then there wouldn't be any trouble. *He* was the only one with the power to create a scandal. As long as he didn't stop the party, and as long as nobody produced evidence of alcohol (and who would?), no damage would be done. Sure, kids would talk about it tomorrow. But the proof was in the punishment. The proof was in the suspensions, the calls to parents. Without punishment, any talk of some wild night would sound like just another stupid AB rumor. Nobody else would believe it. Eventually, it would be forgotten. And Olsen would always have the final word: *The punch wasn't spiked.*

Allison found herself smiling. Now *that* was shrewd. *That* was the way to handle a situation. Yes, sir. That took a certain foresight, a certain kind of leadership. People always made Olsen out to be some kind of fool, but he wasn't. Far from it. She shook her head and walked out the door, but not before giving him an admiring glance.

"Come, come, Antipholus," she said. "We dine too late."

Allison Scott's Seven-Part Life Plan
(with Golden Rule addenda)

1) Go to Princeton with Hobson.

2) Accept Hobson's proposal of marriage while vacationing on the French Riviera.

3) Buy brownstone in Gramercy Park & house in Sag Harbor.

4) Start career as an interior designer, but develop an interest in purebred dogs—specifically rare terriers: Bedlingtons, Cairns, Lakelands

5) Begin torrid affair with a lonely, artsy dog breeder in Greenwich, Connecticut. His name will be something like Dirk. Yes. Definitely Dirk. He'll moonlight as a jazz musician.

6) Break off romance when you realize, once and for all, that Hobson is your true love—and produce a set of gorgeous twin girl children.

7) Start interior design show on the Lifetime Network for Women. Make millions.

GOLDEN RULE #1: REMEMBER YOUR PLACE IN LIFE. PEOPLE ENVY THOSE AT THE TOP.

GOLDEN RULE #2: SOMETHING IS ONLY WORTH DOING IF YOU CAN BECOME FAMOUS FOR IT.

From: Undisclosed Sender
To: Undisclosed Recipient
Subject: Punch
FW was responsible for spiking it. I knew
it. I just found the empty vodka bottles in
the Dumpster outside Ellis. How do you want
to proceed?

From: Undisclosed Sender
To: Undisclosed Recipient
Subject: re: Punch
Carefully. We can't rock the boat too much.
Not with so much at stake. We need him. At
the very least, until after the Carnegie
Mansion exhibition game. We've got a lot of
money riding on him. We should scare him a
little, though. We have to let him know that
he can't screw with us—that we can kick him
out at any time. Or worse. We need to show
him how easy it is. We should set up
something with a patsy, somebody he knows.
Somebody expendable. Maybe even implicate
him, just to make sure he gets the message.

From: Undisclosed Sender
To: Undisclosed Recipient
Subject: re: re: Punch
Understood. I know just the person we can
use. I'll set it up.

Part IV:
The Problem With Being Stuck in the Middle of Nowhere

12

It was finally happening.

Sunday's nightmare was coming true. Faster than she'd expected, actually. This morning, a mere twenty minutes ago, Allison had uttered the very words Sunday had been dreading: *"Sunday, you know, I was thinking. You've been spending an awful lot of time with Fred Wright. Is that really such a great idea?"*

Luckily, Sunday couldn't answer. The hangover was too intense. So she'd just left. But now, as she trudged through the dining hall—a tragic, solitary figure in baggy sweatpants and a gray sweatshirt—the full force of the question struck her. Because it wasn't a question; it was a command. Fred was officially off-limits. Not that Sunday had ever really meant to pursue him (or *had* she?) . . . but still.

The option should have been there, at least.

And from now on she wouldn't even be able to *talk* to him without arousing suspicion. She'd already been found guilty of a crime she hadn't even committed. It was insane. And the most insane part about it was that *she'd seen the whole mess coming.* Yup . . . she'd seen it from the very moment she and Fred had been caught passing notes in Burwell's class.

She shook her head. The dining hall—with its vast sea of circular oak tables and vaulted ceilings and wrought-iron chandeliers—seemed extra cold and gloomy. Or maybe that was just her mood. At least the place was relatively deserted. There were only a few late stragglers, like herself. Good. She didn't want to see anyone else. Her brain was about to burst through her skull. Her tongue had the consistency of an old beach towel.

How do people drink on a regular basis? she wondered.

Actually, it was best not to answer that. Best not to think about drinking. She caught a whiff of fried grease as she grabbed a tray and entered the cafeteria line. *Ugh.* Her stomach squeezed. The harsh fluorescent lights bore down upon her. Normally, she enjoyed Sunday brunch. But today . . . today she would have to forego the scrambled eggs and home fries. Today she would get white toast. Plain white toast. And water.

Jail food.

Right. She smiled sadly as she shoved her tray down the counter, past all the heaping mounds of steaming slop. Jail food. That was fitting. The stone-faced, white-aproned food-service personnel stared at her from the other side of the counter. In four years, she'd never seen them crack a grin. They never so much as said hello. Was the scene here any different, than, say, the scene in the cafeteria at Riker's Island? *Her* life certainly wasn't any different than that of a prisoner. Not anymore.

After picking up her plain white toast, she headed for the drink dispensers. One phrase kept echoing through her mind: *"an awful lot of time."* It was ridiculous. She had spent maybe two hours total with Fred Wright outside of class. Two hours. In two weeks. And *that,* according to some, was "an awful lot of time." Sunday could guess who thought so, too. Oh, yes, she had a theory about where all this information was coming from. Burwell. He watched the two of them like a hawk from his perch at the front of the third-period classroom, staring at them every day as they sat next to each other.

And it didn't matter that they usually split up as soon as they exited the room. The simple fact that they *walked out* together was enough to prompt Burwell to talk to Olsen. Because as far as Burwell was concerned, it meant that Sunday still hadn't learned her lesson, even after being sent to Olsen's office. She was *still* fraternizing with a bad seed like Fred. And that wouldn't do at all. Yes, Sunday could even draw a flow chart of the calls and conversations:

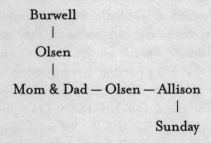

Burwell
|
Olsen
|
Mom & Dad — Olsen — Allison
|
Sunday

She jammed her glass against the water-dispenser lever. She'd been stupid to make that joke with Allison about the wheelbarrow position. *That* was probably the clincher. But she'd been angry. Besides . . .

"Hey, Sunday!"

Well. Speak of the devil. Fred was sitting with Noah at a table in the corner. (And how come nobody made a big deal out of the fact that *Noah* hung out with Fred? Wasn't *he* an AB, as well?) Fred smiled. Noah smiled, too—but only half-heartedly. He looked pretty much the way Sunday felt. His face was pale and puffy. Dark circles ringed his eyes.

"Come here," Fred called. He waved her over.

For the briefest instant, she actually found herself hesitating. But then she thought: *screw it.* So what if people saw her eating with Fred? She'd already been burned at the figurative stake. There was no point in trying to put out the fire now. She marched right over and slammed her tray down on the table, then slumped into the seat beside Fred.

"What's up, guys?" she said.

Fred's smile widened. "Did you have fun last night?" he asked.

She shot a quick glance at Noah. "Uh . . . yeah," she said cautiously. "Not too bad."

"I hear it was pretty wild," Fred said.

Sunday took a sip of water. "Is that what Noah told you?"

"Well, yeah." Fred picked up his fork and absently pushed some food around on his plate. "But I probably could have guessed as much. You know, what with the punch and all."

Sunday stared at him. "What do you mean?"

He met her gaze. There was a twinkle in his eye. "Vodka usually spices up a party."

"Oh, my God," Sunday whispered. Delight swept over her, flushing away the dank cobwebs of the hangover. "It was *you.*"

Fred shrugged.

She started laughing. "How did you do it?"

"You really think I'm gonna divulge any trade secrets to _you_?" he asked, arching one eyebrow. "A member of the student council? Someone hand-picked to uphold the rules—"

"Give me a break." She was starting to feel that tingle again.

He sighed. "Well, all right. See, I—"

"Sunday!"

_Oh, no._ That shriek. Sunday glanced over her shoulder. The tingle vanished. The hangover returned, full-force.

Allison had tracked her here. She stormed right up to the table. She was still wearing the oversized T-shirt she'd slept in. And a pair of five-hundred-dollar Capri pants.

"What are you doing?" she demanded, planting herself directly behind Sunday's chair.

"Hey, Allison," Noah said brightly. "How's it going?"

Allison ignored him. "Sunday, why did you ditch me this morning?"

"Because I wanted some breakfast," she muttered, turning back to the table. She picked up a piece of toast and tore off a chunk with her teeth.

"Why don't you join us?" Fred suggested.

Sunday grinned as she chewed. She wished she

had a mirror. She would love to see Allison's expression right now.

"I'm not hungry," Allison stated. Her voice was clipped.

Noah pointed at a glass. "Thirsty? You could join us for a beverage."

"I want to talk to *Sunday*," Allison growled. "I want to continue the conversation we started this morning. We were discussing . . ."

Footsteps drowned out the rest of her speech.

Sunday glanced over her shoulder again.

Oh, brother. It was Tony Viverito. He was glowering at Fred.

"I want a rematch," Tony announced when he reached the table. He slung his book bag off his shoulder and onto the floor. Sunday almost laughed. Jocks were a frighteningly predictable breed. Well, except for Fred.

Fred sighed. He tried to smile, but he looked pained. "Can't we just—"

"Today. Two o'clock."

"Why? Look, man, I don't want to play with you."

Tony sneered. "I thought you said you *did*."

"Well, I changed my mind, all right—"

"Viverito!" a voice barked.

Sunday turned for a third time.

Now Mr. Burwell was barreling toward them. *Jesus.*

What was this, a convention? Today's double-breasted suit was navy blue. For some reason, Burwell looked just as pissed as Tony and Allison. His usually expressionless, frog-like face was twisted in a grimace. He was probably hung over, too. He'd downed more than a couple of cups of punch himself.

"Viverito!" he repeated. "Don't move!"

Sunday rubbed her temples. All these people were yelling far too loudly.

Tony's eyes narrowed. "I'm not moving," he said.

"You and your girlfriend were just on a little forage into the woods," Burwell stated. "I saw you coming from the Arts Center. And neither of you are artists. Am I right?"

A little forage. Another Burwellism for Noah's list. Unfortunately, Sunday was just a little too tense and miserable to find any humor in it. She shot a quick glance at Noah and Fred. Noah was staring at his plate. Fred was glaring at Burwell. The rest of the dining hall was starting to whisper, to turn toward their table. Not that she could blame them. It was a circus over here. Thank God there weren't that many people around.

"So what if I was coming from the Arts Center?" Tony asked.

Burwell thrust a finger at the floor near Tony's feet. "Let me see your book bag."

Tony frowned. "Why?"

"Open your book bag," Burwell growled. He snatched the knapsack off the floor.

"Hey!" Tony protested. "What are you doing?"

Burwell didn't answer. He simply tore open the zipper, grunting. Sunday could feel her face getting hot. What *was* this, the Gestapo? Since when did teachers descend upon students and search their bags without asking? It wasn't just weird, it was *wrong. . . .*

"I didn't know it was a crime to carry around a book bag," Tony grumbled. "For your information, I was planning on going to the library—"

"I *knew* it!" Burwell snapped.

He snatched something out of the bag, then dropped the bag back on the floor. It landed with an unceremonious thud. Clutched in Burwell's chubby fingers was a small, circular metal tin. The words "Old Hickory" were printed on its side.

Sunday blinked. *Wait a second.* Tony didn't chew that stuff. He'd said it made him barf.

Her eyes shot to Fred, who looked absolutely bewildered. His jaw hung slack.

"That's not *mine!*" Tony cried.

Mr. Burwell snorted. "Sure. You're just holding it for a friend, huh?"

Tony shook his head violently. "I swear to God. I don't chew tobacco—"

"Come with me," Mr. Burwell interrupted. "Right now." He took Tony's arm and dragged him away from the table. Tony seemed to be too shocked to resist. *Good Lord.* Sunday cringed. Her brain couldn't handle this. It was way too intense for a Sunday morning, much less a hangover. She wished she could crawl under the table and disappear. . . .

"Hey!" Fred shouted. He jumped to his feet, nearly knocking his chair. His face was red with rage. "Mr. Burwell! Didn't you hear what he just said? Tony doesn't chew tobacco. So there must be some kind of mistake."

"He doesn't chew tobacco, eh?" Burwell barked, stopping in his tracks and spinning around. "So what are you saying, Wright? Is it *yours*, then? Did you sneak it in there? Are you trying to frame him?"

Fred gaped at him. "*What*? Of course not—"

"So stay out of this. Unless you want some *real* trouble."

Before Fred could say another word, Mr. Burwell escorted Tony through the dining hall and disappeared out the big set of double doors. They clanged shut behind him.

Nobody spoke. Sunday swallowed. Noah stared intently at his plate, as if it might somehow magically deliver him from the table.

"Di-di-did you *see* that?" Fred finally sputtered. "That was *insane!*"

Sunday nodded, gazing up at him. She wasn't nodding in mutual outrage at the injustice that had just taken place. Well, yes, partly. But she was also nodding because she suddenly realized what had happened. In spite of the fact that she was in a daze, in spite of all the shouting and weirdness, she was able to see the truth. Fred had just put himself on the line for someone else. Someone he didn't even like. Someone who hated him. Just for the sake of doing the right thing, the *moral* thing. He'd performed an act of pure kindness that she never would have. And sure, it hadn't worked, but . . .

There was a tap on Sunday's shoulder.

"So?" Allison asked. "Are we going to continue the conversation we started earlier, or not?"

Sunday sagged in her chair.

Oh, Allison. In that instant, with that one question, she'd trampled Sunday's swell of emotion, as swiftly as if she'd blown out a candle. And she didn't even know it.

"Or not," Sunday murmured sadly. She took another bite of toast.

Memo from Coach Watts to all students on the Varsity Basketball team

To: The Wessex Warriors (V)
From: Coach Watts
Date: 10/2
Re: Probation

Warriors:

As some of you know, Tony Viverito was expelled over the weekend for violation of probation, due to an incident involving possession of chewing tobacco. It might behoove some of you to take a look at the orientation handbook, specifically page 86—the rules re: tobacco products. The entire school would be terribly disappointed if we let this season slip away due to immaturity and poor judgment.

As a result of this unfortunate turn of events, I have decided to place all of you on probation. I know this may seem unfair. Why should the actions of one bad apple affect all your lives? But I wouldn't look at this as a punishment. Just a gentle reminder to stay in line. Remember: If you don't break the rules, probation doesn't mean anything. It doesn't go on your record. Colleges won't know anything about it.

Unless you break the rules.

I trust I won't be hearing any of your names in conjunction with tobacco again.

cc: Phillip Olsen, Paul Burwell

13

"I'm telling you, man," Fred muttered. "Something weird is going on."

Noah had never seen Fred chew this much Old Hickory. He looked like he had the mumps. He kept pacing around the Waldorf, spitting huge wads of brown phlegm into the dirt. He'd come dangerously close to hitting Noah a couple of times. Not that he'd noticed. Fred's mind was clearly in some other place. The fact that he'd agreed to come to the Waldorf just before dinner—or even to the Waldorf at *all*—went a long way to showing what kind of funk he was in. Fred was strictly a Marriott guy now, ever since that first day of school, when Allison had told him to get lost.

"I really think you shouldn't stress about it so

much," Noah said. "There's nothing you can do. It wasn't your fault. Right?"

"But it *was* my fault," Fred said. He stopped for a moment and peered into the darkening woods. "I mean, not literally. It's just . . . I know Tony doesn't dip. He *told* me. He's like you; dip makes him barf. And the thing is, he was caught with the *same brand* of tobacco I have. Old Hickory. So, in a way, it looks like what Burwell said. It almost looks like *I* planted it on him."

Noah didn't say anything. He stared at the ground. He couldn't argue with that. It *did* sort of look as though Fred had planted the tobacco on Tony. As a matter of fact, Noah had considered that very possibility many times in the past few days. But Fred wasn't . . . evil.

Or was he?

No. No way. Noah just couldn't bring himself to believe it. He liked Fred. And sure, Fred might have played a little dirty on the basketball court, but that was just a game. Besides, Fred didn't have any reason to get rid of Tony; he was clearly a superior basketball player, so Tony posed no threat to him.

On the other hand . . .

Tony *had* pissed him off on numerous occasions. And Fred had mentioned the fact that Tony's brother, Salvatore, was Fred's ex-girlfriend's boyfriend. Or something. (Noah remembered Salvatore; he was two years older—quiet and chubby, a redhead like Tony. People called him 'The Beard.' He had been the only kid at Wessex who had a full beard—which had led to rumors that he took steroids and was actually in his late twenties.)

More to the point, though: When it came down to it, Noah didn't know Fred that well. At all. Fred was capable of pulling some pretty wild stunts. The guy had spiked the student council punch, after all. Not that this was a bad thing. But still.

"I know Burwell had something to do with this," Fred muttered. "He has a key to my room. He stole my La-Z-Boy. So he must have gone through my room when I wasn't there and seen what kind of tobacco I chew, then bought some and slipped it into Tony's bag. . . ."

Please drop it, Noah groaned silently.

Five days had already passed since Tony had been booted. Yes, it was a tragedy. But Fred needed to stop talking about it, particularly if he wanted to clear himself of any involvement. Noah understood obsession very well, but this . . . this wasn't healthy.

For some unfathomable reason, Fred kept harping on a bizarre theory: that Burwell knew he was a troublemaker but couldn't expel him because he was a basketball star, so instead Burwell was scaring Fred into good behavior by getting one of his teammates expelled.

Noah couldn't even follow it. Burwell wasn't smart enough to come up with a plan that complicated. He was smart enough to dispose of a La-Z-Boy, and that was about it. But planting chewing tobacco on Tony Viverito to scare Fred? It made no sense. Fred was starting to sound like Mackenzie, actually. Noah should get *her* to listen to this crap. She'd love it. It would be another piece in the big Wessex conspiracy puzzle.

Hmm. That might not be a bad idea, actually—putting Fred and Mackenzie together. Not only would it get Fred off *his* back for a while (every friend/tutor/mentor needed a break now and then), but it would distract Fred from Sunday.

" . . . and you know how I *know* it was Burwell?" Fred was asking. "How I *know* it?"

"No, Fred," Noah mumbled. "How do you know it was Burwell?"

Fred spit again. "Because Winslow Ellis never sold Tony a tin of Old Hickory." He turned and fixed Noah with an intense stare—as if that comment were somehow supposed to be of deep significance. "I asked Winslow Ellis specifically: Did you sell a tin to Tony? And he said no. So where else would Tony have gotten it, huh? There *is* no other guy to buy it from."

"Maybe he went into town," Noah said.

"He went all the way into town to buy something that makes him barf?" Fred cried.

"Fred, come on. Maybe he wanted to give it another try. Maybe he saw how you chewed it and decided, what the hell. Maybe he thought it would make him a better basketball player. Maybe he wanted to give it to you as a peace offering."

Fred didn't even smile. He just shook his head and turned back to the woods. "No way, man. No way. This has Burwell written all over it. I mean, the guy is relentless. *You* were the one who told me about the enemies list, remember? He's been watching me from the second I got here. I bet he followed Winnie and me here that first day of school. That's how he knew we were lighting fires. . . ."

Noah looked at the ground again. He'd been kidding about the enemies list. Fred was starting to lose his sense of humor. And that was bad. But that wasn't even the biggest problem. No, the biggest problem was that some of this nonsense was actually starting to rub off on Noah. The more Fred talked about it, the more weirdly acceptable it *did* seem. Noah swallowed. What if somebody were to frame *him*? If a faculty member (Burwell or whomever) could interfere with a student's life so easily, if Wessex could expel a kid on a whim . . . but no. That would never happen to Noah. He was an AB. A *legacy*. Wessex needed him. And, sad to say—even though Noah had nothing against the guy—Tony Viverito didn't carry the same cachet as he did.

"You know what I'm thinking?" Fred said. "I'm thinking Burwell is somebody's thug."

"Thug?" Noah managed a weak laugh. "Have you been hanging out with Hobson?"

Fred finally cracked a grin. "No, seriously." He spit again—firing a pellet of tobacco that whizzed within inches of Noah's knee. "He's like . . . a strong-man. For someone else."

"For who?" Noah asked.

"I don't know. Whoever's in charge. Olsen."

"Olsen? Oh, boy. Now you sound like Mackenzie."

"How do I sound like Mackenzie?"

"She thinks that Olsen is the evil ringleader, too." Noah shook his head. "I guess it goes back to that old saying: It's always the person you least suspect."

"Well, tell me this. How does a moron like Burwell keep a job for twenty years—" Fred broke off at some movement in the woods.

Somebody was joining their little party. Sunday, maybe? Noah craned his neck. Nope. Winnie. His shoulders slumped.

"What's up, dudes?" Winnie called. He smiled at Noah. "I've been looking all over for you. I've got something for you."

Noah frowned. "What? A ten-dollar notebook?"

"Very funny." Winnie dug into his pocket as he reached the clearing and pulled out a crumpled note. "Miss Burke asked me to give this to you."

For a moment, Noah just stared at it.

He turned to Fred. Fred was frowning, too.

"Miss Burke asked you to pass me a note," Noah finally muttered. "How gullible do you think I am?"

Winnie shook his head. "I'm telling you the truth. She stopped me outside the Humanities building about a half hour ago." He thrust the note toward Noah's hand.

Noah didn't take it. "What's it say?" he asked.

"How the hell should I know?"

"Come on, dude." Noah smirked. "If Miss Burke really did give you this note, then I *know* you would have read it. I would have."

Winnie smiled. "She wants you to come to her house."

Noah snatched the paper from Winnie's fingers.

Dear Noah,

I just wanted to apologize for my inappropriate behavior the night of the student council dinner. I must have had too

*much wine. I'd like to talk to you, if you have the chance.
I'll be at home all evening. I'm the dorm adviser in Meade
Hall, in case you don't know.*

*Sincerely,
Miss Burke*

Okay. This was obviously a prank. Except . . .
Noah didn't recognize the handwriting. It wasn't
Winnie's. On the other hand, Winnie might easily
be an expert forger, in addition to his other criminal talents. Noah's heart thumped a little faster.
Was this for real? He could find out, of course. He
could go to Meade Hall. What was the worst that
could happen? He would show this note to her, and
she would tell him she didn't write it. They'd share
an embarrassed laugh. And she'd slam the door in
his face. No harm, no foul.

"What's it say?" Fred asked.

"I'm not really sure," Noah said.

Meade Hall, like Ellis, was one of those cute
Victorian-style mansions on the outskirts of campus—a
former home that had been converted into a dormitory
for five sophomore girls. It figured that Miss Burke had
been assigned to live there. Being a dorm adviser for five
sophomores was a typical, low-pressure gig for a new
teacher. Two years down the road, Miss Burke would

probably be transferred to Arcadia, the big freshman girls' dorm—where she would be responsible for twenty homesick, screechy, barely pubescent females.

If she lasted that long, of course.

She would have to learn a thing or two if she wanted any kind of long-term career at Wessex. Like how the administration generally frowned on secret note-passing between teachers and students.

Noah hesitated on the dark path, staring up at the cozy lights of the dorm. He'd deliberately waited until after dark to come here. Why, though, he wasn't quite sure. He shivered. A crisp breeze rustled his hair. It was starting to get cold at night. He glanced down at his watch. Nine-fifteen. That gave him forty-five minutes to . . . well, to talk with Miss Burke about whatever she wanted to talk about. Check-in was at ten o'clock on a school night. Of course, an exception could be made if a student was meeting with a teacher. Theoretically, Noah could stay here as long as he wanted—provided that Miss Burke alerted Burwell to Noah's whereabouts.

If the note wasn't a forgery. *If* this wasn't a prank.

Noah's heart started thumping again.

Okay. Better get this over with. He headed down a little cobbled walkway to a side door tucked behind the trees, the door to the faculty apartment. And at that moment, he realized why he'd waited so long to come here. He'd been procrastinating. He was terrified. He had no idea what to expect. Why would *she* apologize to *him*? He was the one who'd insisted that she do a dance he'd invented called the "wang-dang-doodle," which consisted pretty much only of pelvic thrusts, done completely out of time. . . .

Forgery. It's just a forgery.

He drew in his breath and knocked.

"Who is it?" Miss Burke called.

"It's . . . ah, Noah, Miss Burke. Noah Percy."

A moment later, the door opened.

Noah smiled awkwardly. He hoped she wouldn't ask him to shake hands. His palms were moist. . . .

Jesus. Miss Burke was *crying.*

Or she had been. Or she'd just finished crying. Her eyes were puffy, and her cheeks were wet. Her dark hair hung in her face. Her clothes were completely disheveled. She was wearing capri pants and an oversized white oxford shirt, a man's shirt—but it was barely buttoned. He could see her bra. He tried not to look at it.

"Um . . . I can come back later," he mumbled. "If this is a bad time—"

"No, no." She sniffled and forced a smile. "Sorry. It's nothing. I'm glad you came. Winslow gave you my note, right?"

Noah's pulse doubled.

"Are *you* all right?" she asked.

"Uh . . . fine," he croaked, nodding several times.

She sniffed again. "Come in."

So the note wasn't a forgery. *It wasn't a forgery.* Noah's knees turned to jelly. He followed her into the little apartment. She'd done it up in a very funky, college sort of way: candles, lots of plants, a ratty old beige couch . . . and a coffee-stained piece of plywood on top of a trunk for a makeshift coffee table. The Beatles were playing softly in the background. It was a song from *Sergeant Pepper's:* "When I'm 64." Classy. Noah loved that song.

A bottle of wine sat on the table. So did a full wineglass. The bottle was nearly empty.

Miss Burke sat down on the couch.

Noah smiled at her. He wondered if she could hear his heart pounding. The only other place to sit, aside from the floor, was on the couch beside her.

"Have a seat," she said. She scooted over to make room for him. Then she picked up the glass and took a long, slow sip.

As Noah sat down (and he was very relieved to do so, because his legs were about to give out from under him), he reflected upon the potential significance of this wine-drinking. According to the note, Miss Burke had invited him here to apologize for her behavior . . . *due to too much wine.* Of course, the student council zaniness hadn't been a result of wine at all; it had been a result of spiked punch—but that wasn't really the point.

Now, obviously, she was in a bad state. But still, she hadn't even bothered to put away the wine. And she'd been *expecting* him. The note had said she'd be at home all evening. If Noah had gone to Burwell's apartment, say, and Burwell was drinking a beer, there was no doubt in Noah's mind that Burwell would stop drinking. Not that there was any rule against drinking in front of students; faculty members did it all the time at those Opening Day parties—yet to do it so brazenly, in this kind of situation . . . it just seemed a little . . .

"Are you sure you're all right, Noah?" Miss Burke asked.

He nodded. "Fine." He couldn't bring himself to look at her. Instead, he stared at a sickly plant on the windowsill. "How about you? Are *you* all right?"

She laughed softly. "No. Not really." She put the glass back on the table. It was empty.

"You know, I really could come back some other time—"

"No, no. Stay. Please. I'm sorry."

Noah swallowed, then turned to her. She smiled. He caught a glimpse of her bra again: a strip of navy-blue Lycra against her white skin. He turned back to the plant. He was going to have a heart attack. What a sordid way to end his short life. "Student Suffers

Coronary in Teacher's Apartment. Cause of Death Linked to Brassiere." Oh, well. He supposed he should make the most of what little time he had left.

"Um . . . do you want, um—to talk about it?" he offered.

"That's sweet," she murmured. "But I don't think it would be fair of me to dump my problems on a seventeen-year-old boy."

He shook his head, staring at the plant as if it were a lifeboat, an antidote for poison—his only chance for survival. "No, no, no," he said. "Don't let the looks fool you. A lot of people don't know this, but I'm really thirty-five. It's just that, uh . . . see, I sold my soul to Satan when I was a kid—you know, in exchange for eternal youth. And it's really worked out great. I mean, the only problem is . . . uh, you know, zits. And eternal damnation."

Miss Burke laughed again. "How do you do that?" she asked.

"Do what?" he mumbled.

"How do you say the funniest things, and make everybody forget their problems?" She reached for the bottle of wine.

Blood surged to Noah's face. "I . . . uh, well, see . . . some-something about being around faculty members compels me to tell outrageous lies," he stammered. *The plant. Look at the plant. The plant is your savior.* "You know, I just find myself talking—you know, like in your class, or in Headmaster Olsen's office, or with Mr. Burwell, or here—and the lies just start adding up, and I kind of run with it. It's like I can't stop, and I'm just watching myself, and listening to myself construct these intricate, idiotic—"

"Noah," she whispered. She poured herself another glass, finishing the bottle.

He swallowed again. "Yes?"

"If I'm going to dump my problems on you, I can't have you thinking of me as a member of the faculty. Not at this moment. In class, yes. But not here. Not now."

That was it. Forget the bra. He turned to her. She *was* a member of the faculty. Sure, she was new. So maybe she didn't quite get it. Maybe she didn't quite understand that she was an authority figure. But more than that, she was a *woman*. An *adult*. She had a whole host of issues and concerns that Noah couldn't even *conceive* of. Taxes. Credit history. The right to vote. Student loan payments. Birth control. He couldn't relate to any of that. She was right: She *shouldn't* dump her problems on a seventeen-year-old boy. The difference between seventeen and twenty-two was monumental. It was an unbridgeable chasm. . . .

"It's just that I didn't realize that I'd get so lonely out here," she breathed. She averted her eyes and sipped the wine, cupping the glass with both hands.

"Lonely?" Noah asked. His voice cracked.

She didn't seem to notice, though. She just nodded, staring off into space. "I mean, I went to college not too far from here. I know what it's like to be stuck in the middle of nowhere." She smiled wistfully. "Nothing to do except tip cows. But back at college, there were people I could *share* things with. There were friends, peers, boyfriends. . . ." Her voice faded. "I don't have anyone here. This will probably sound pathetic to you, but *you're* the only one who comes close to being a friend. You're the only one I look forward to talking to. And I don't even know you that well."

Noah blinked. "That . . . uh, that doesn't sound pathetic to me," he heard himself say.

She placed the wine back on the table. She seemed to be moving in slow motion. Noah's ears filled with a strange rushing sound. His skin burned. He couldn't even hear the Beatles anymore; he could hear nothing but the furious beating of his own pulse: *dum-dum-dum-dum* . . . She turned to him. Her eyes were heavily lidded. He saw now that her irises were green—a very clear, almost glass-like green.

"I'd like to get to know you better," she whispered.

He nodded. "Me, too."

He found himself drifting toward her. Her ivory

face filled his entire field of vision. It was as if he had no control over his body; he was simply a moth being drawn to a great, big, beautiful lightbulb. And a thought flitted through his brain—the last thought before the synapses stopped firing and that particular organ shut down completely. *Fred was right.* Maybe there was a full moon, or the planets were in some kind of strange alignment, or somebody had put LSD in the school meatloaf. But something weird *was* going on.

Of course, everybody could use a little weirdness now and then.

A Segment of Noah Percy's Wesleyan Application

Part 3: In two hundred words or less, describe an incident you regret, and the lesson you learned from it.

I Know That Sleeping With a Teacher Was Wrong, But She's Hot

It's the old boarding school daydream, the subject of countless films and pulp novels. A male student fantasizes about being seduced by a young, sexy, female teacher . . . and it comes true.

But what if it were to happen in real life?

Well, it happened to me last night. And I'm still trying to figure it out. It certainly has nothing to do with my appearance. I enclose a picture as evidence.

The moral implications are myriad and obvious. Sleeping with a teacher is, objectively, reprehensible. It will most likely damage our student–teacher dynamic. Then there's the matter of law: She can be held criminally liable for statutory rape. And since I am still maturing, since I am still developing socially and otherwise, there is an unfortunate possibility that I will develop an unhealthy obsession with her—one that leads to my becoming her stalker.

But I don't regret our encounter for any of these reasons. (Nor will I stalk her, in case you were worried.) I simply gave in to the moment. I regret I did not have more self-control, because I wanted to surrender my virginity to someone I truly love—that someone being a fellow senior, a girl I have known my entire life. And now that will never happen. I've lost a dream I've had since I first became a student at Wessex.

Oh, well. Like I said, this teacher is hot. She's a twenty-two-year-old bombshell. That counts for something, I suppose.

14

Was it unethical to go through another person's garbage can?

Well, no. No, it wasn't. Not if you cared about that person.

Besides, this wasn't technically a "garbage can." It was a custom-made, black titanium Sven Larsen waste receptacle. This particular model was known as The Obelisk. It was a simple cylinder, for white paper only. Allison bent over and peered into it. Sven Larsen had stressed that The Obelisk was not to be soiled with gum, candy-wrappers, or even used Kleenex. His furnishings were works of art. His waste receptacles were meant strictly for clean recyclables.

Of course, Sunday didn't seem to care about that. Typical. Allison's jaw tightened. Nope, Sunday's Sven

Larsen Obelisk was stuffed to the rim with wadded-up foil, a couple of paper cups (with traces of juice still inside!), and something that looked like old American cheese. So. That made it *doubly* okay for Allison to look through it. She owed it to Sven Larsen to purge his titanium of impurity, and she owed it to the Winthrops to ascertain whether or not Sunday was still trying to pursue a relationship with Fred Wright.

Right. Time to get to work. Of course, there *was* the ickiness factor . . . but what the hell. She'd use gloves. That pair of last year's Burberrys. Her mom had picked them up at a sample sale. They could definitely be sacrificed for a good cause.

Allison tiptoed back across the little common area to her own room. She stole a quick peek into the hall, just to be safe. But, no—Sunday and Mackenzie had gone to dinner. They wouldn't be back for another half hour. After sunset. Still, she'd leave the door open a crack. Just to hear any footsteps coming. One could never be too cautious. She darted into her room and rummaged through her bureau for the gloves. Ah, yes. Right under the scarves. These gloves were perfect. Too loose, and too ugly. And gray. No way she'd wear these in public. She pulled them on and tiptoed back to Sunday's room.

I really hope I don't find anything, Sunday, she thought to herself. *I really do.*

Her face shriveled as she kneeled beside the black cylinder. She would have to be quick about this, or she might gag. In and out. Keeping her face as far away from the garbage as possible, she reached in and started digging through it. There were some crumpled up papers in here, but they were near the bottom. . . .

"Eww!" she cried.

Something had *dripped* on her. A little trickle of juice. Disgusting. She'd definitely have to hop into the shower the second she was finished. Okay . . . okay . . . *here* was something suspicious. A piece of notebook paper mashed into a little ball no bigger than a plum. Allison yanked it out and unfolded it. Her eyes narrowed. It looked like . . . a letter. Some of the words were smudged, but she could still make out the majority:

just think it's so cool what you tried to do for Tony. And it's strange, because when I was walking into the dining hall that morning, I was feeling so sorry for myself—thinking about how powerless I was, about how everybody else always seems to make my decisions FOR me. But when I saw what you did for Tony, I realized that I'm the only one to blame for that. I mean, the reason I feel trapped is because I've always been scared of taking risks, to stand up and do what's right.

But you don't seem to have that problem.

I don't even know why what you did in the dining hall affected me so much. It just did. For some reason, it was one of those defining moments. I mean, everybody should experience one profound moment in their lives, one event when—BOOM!—their flight to Tokyo crashes, and they save the lives of six strangers on a snowy mountainside, and so they decide to become paramedics or doctors. You know, instead of investment bankers. Does that make any sense?

Probably not. Anyway, now comes the hard part. Brace yourself. What I'm going to say next is going to sound a little off-the-wall. I guess that's why I'm writing to you. People can hide behind letters. If they regret what they've written, they can just say, "Oh, I was in a really weird mood when I wrote that. That wasn't really me. That isn't really the way I feel." But this IS the way I feel, no matter what I may say or do in the future.

So this is it: I want to spend some time with you. I want to get to know you better.

My God, that looks even more horrible and cheesy written down than the way it sounded in my head. Whatever. I don't care. I had to say it. I'm tired of hiding and lying. Allison (and everyone else) says I shouldn't hang out with you, but it doesn't matter. And maybe it won't even lead to anything. Maybe we'll end up being casual friends, or best buddies, or even enemies. But I'd like the chance to find out—on MY terms, without anybody telling me what I should do.

I guess I'm telling you all this because I hope you feel at least partially the same.

Sunday

Allison's hands shook. She scanned the letter again. Then a third time. She was grinding her teeth so hard that her gums began to ache. But she couldn't stop. The situation . . . *My God.* It was worse than she'd ever dreamed. If this letter was in the garbage, then it must have been a rough draft. She could only imagine what the *final* version was like. Did it include explicit sexual fantasies? A marriage proposal? More back-stabbing vitriol at Allison's expense?

Oh, of course. Allison was *sure* about that part. No doubt Sunday was bad-mouthing her *true* friend (her sister, practically!) to her new soul mate, Fred Wright. Why not? It certainly fit with everything else. Allison shook her head. She couldn't look at these words any-more. They were too pitiful, too disturbing. . . .

Voices.

Mackenzie and Sunday. They were coming up the stairs. Allison could hear them laughing. *Dammit.*

What were they doing back? They couldn't have eaten *that* fast. She jumped to her feet—but her knee struck The Obelisk. It went toppling over, landing with a loud clang. Allison winced. Her heart lurched. *Oh, no, no, no.* Cups were rolling onto the floor. Little drops of juice were splattering everywhere. She crouched down and tried to sweep up the cups, but she was still holding the letter . . . her entire body was trembling. She couldn't think; she was too panicked. Best just to get the cylinder upright first . . .

"Allison?"

Too late. She whirled on the balls of her feet—still huddled on the ground, garbage everywhere, still clutching . . . *the letter.* In a Burberry sample-sale glove.

Mackenzie and Sunday stood in the doorway of the suite, staring at her, bewildered.

"What are you doing?" Sunday asked. She stepped toward her bedroom.

"I . . . I was just coming to look for something in here, and I . . . um, I accidentally kicked over your trashcan," she stammered. She forced a smile, simultaneously stuffing the letter back where it belonged.

Sunday's forehead wrinkled. "Why are you wearing gloves?"

"I . . . I . . ." Allison couldn't think of an excuse. She was too frightened.

Sunday was hovering right over her now. She

squinted into the Sven Larsen Obelisk. Her eyes zeroed in on the letter. Her face suddenly went slack.

"Oh, my God," she whispered. "You were going through my garbage—"

"No, no," Allison protested, standing up. "I swear I wasn't—"

"You read that letter I wrote," Sunday interrupted. Oddly enough, though, she didn't even seem that upset. Her face was a tad pale, but that was it. "You went through my garbage and read a letter I wrote to somebody else."

Allison shook her head. "Sunday, I swear . . ." But she knew there was no point in lying. "Okay, I did read the letter—but, look, I was just doing it for your own good, and there's—"

"My own good," Sunday interrupted. She laughed—a harsh, bitter, little laugh. "You know what's funny, Al? I'm sure you actually believe that." She turned and marched back toward the suite door, right past Mackenzie.

Mackenzie glanced between the two of them, chewing her lip.

"Sunday, wait!" Allison called. "We have to talk. You can't just—"

"Talk?" Sunday paused at the door and glanced over her shoulder. "About what? There's nothing to talk about. If you can't see how wrong and twisted and sick it is to go through somebody's garbage, to read their personal letters behind their backs . . ." She started blinking. "I . . . I just can't live like this anymore." Her voice quavered. Her eyes were watering. "I can't do it. I'm sorry."

Allison swallowed. A spasm of guilt shot through her. "Sunday, please," she murmured.

"Yeah, come on, Sunday," Mackenzie pleaded. "Just listen to what Allison has to say."

Sunday shook her head. "I can't do it," she repeated. And with that, she left the suite, slamming the door behind her.

October 6

Dear Mr. and Mrs. Winthrop,

How are you? I hope all is well.

By now you've probably heard all about the little tiff Sunday and I had tonight. And I hope by the time you receive this letter, we will have long since made amends. Anyway, I just want to state, for the record, that I was NOT going through Sunday's garbage, despite what she may have told you. She had written a letter and put it into a recycling bin, where it was lying on top of a lot of other papers in plain view. I was on my way to take these recyclables to the Dumpster outside our dorm, and I just happened to catch a glimpse of what was on the page in question. Naturally, I was concerned. Sunday had written a rather lurid love letter to Fred Wright. Apparently, despite all our efforts, she refuses to listen to us.

If there's anything you'd like me to do, please let me know. And I want you both to know, whatever happens, I'm here for your daughter.

Love,
Allison

235

Part V:
"You Came to Booticize My Booty."

15

"Drastic times call for drastic measures."

Was that how the saying went? Or maybe it was: "Desperate times call for desperate measures." Yeah, that sounded more like it. Or maybe—

Whatever. Mackenzie couldn't remember. And it didn't make any difference, because this measure was both desperate *and* drastic. But she had to do it. If Allison could go through Sunday's garbage in order to save their friendship—well, then, Mackenzie could go to Hobson and demand that he get back together with Allison.

It *had* to be done.

Mackenzie had given the matter a lot of thought. More than usual. In the three hours that had passed since she and Sunday had caught Allison in Sunday's garbage, Mackenzie had methodically searched her memory for the root of their collective woes. And she kept coming back to the same answer: It had all started when Hobson dumped Allison. First the redecorating. Then the temper flares. Then this whole business with the letter. *Poor, poor Allison.* She was on the verge of a full-fledged breakdown.

And Mackenzie had to stop it.

She wrapped her arms around herself, gripping *Past Life Regression Therapy* tightly as she marched down the deserted path toward Logan Hall, Hobson's dorm. The cold night air fueled her pace. She was crisp. Alert. Ready for action. It was nearly nine o'clock. That gave her an hour to hypnotize Hobson, sift through his PLH, pinpoint the problem, then explain to him in no uncertain terms that he was destined—no, *preordained*—to be with Allison for his entire life. *This* life, anyway.

The arched roof of Logan Hall loomed over her. She didn't relish coming here. Logan was definitely one of the creepiest buildings on campus. It was made of old stone, with this medieval vibe, like a haunted house. Loners lived here. Winnie lived here. There were no doubles, only singles. It was definitely a focus of spiritual energy, both negative and positive.

Of course, such energy would certainly facilitate the therapy.

Yes. She blew through the front door and hesitated for a moment in the warmth of the front hall, debating whether or not she should ask Mr. Wendt for permission to visit. But, no. Best just to sneak up to Hobson's room. No risk of being disturbed that way. Mr. Wendt was too nosy.

Hobson will go for this, she told herself as she tiptoed up to the second floor. Sure, he would. He was an open-minded sort of guy. He embraced new ideas. He'd embraced rap, hadn't he? Even now, she could hear hip-hop thumping from his room, all the way down the hall. *Wow.* That was loud. The closer she got, the more she could feel it in her teeth. Especially the bass. Hobson's door rattled on its hinges.

She knocked three times loudly, keeping a wary eye out for Mr. Wendt.

The volume dropped.

"Who is it?" Hobson asked from inside.

"Mackenzie," she whispered.

He threw the door open. "Yo, wassup, Mack?"

She blushed. He didn't have any pants on. Just plaid boxer shorts and a T-shirt with the words: "Tupac Shakur R.I.P." And some kind of red handkerchief-type-thingy on his head.

He poked his head into the hall and glanced toward the stairs. "Didn't get permission, huh? Right on." He grabbed her jacket sleeve and yanked her inside, closing the door behind him. "So what brings you to the Mack-A-Lot crib?"

"I . . . uh . . ." She couldn't focus. She was having a hard time concentrating. But it wasn't because he was half-naked. His "crib" . . . it looked like the set of a Dr. Dre video. Last year, he'd had a few posters, but this year, he'd spared no expense. Not an inch of wall space was left uncovered. Malt liquor posters, "Wu Wear" posters . . . He had a leopard-skin comforter. And a pair of turntables—*real* ones, the kind an actual DJ would use. She'd never seen a turntable up close. They were big. The speakers were the size of bookcases. Sven Larsen would have a *fit* if he ever saw this place.

"Make yourself at home, yo," he said.

Mackenzie couldn't even move. She was speechless.

Hobson stretched out on the comforter. "You know, I was hoping you'd pay me a visit, Mack," he said, grinning. "I had my sights set on you. And when Mack-A-Lot's gunnin', the honeys come runnin'."

She shook her head. She couldn't follow him. "What?" she asked.

He raised his eyebrows. "You came to get some-a-this, yo. Don't deny it."

"Some of . . . what?"

"Some-a-*this*." He sat up straight and tapped his

chest. "Some-a-Mack-A-Lot! You came to booti-cize my booty. You came to get freaky."

Mackenzie shook her head again. "I'm sorry . . . I can't understand you."

"Baby, I'm kicking the straight-up truth!"

She frowned. "About *what*?"

Hobson laughed suddenly. "You're a cutie, Mack. You know that?" He slipped into a Hispanic accent. "'There is no lying in you,'" he quoted.

It was a line from *Scarface*. Mackenzie could feel herself blushing again. She was beginning to get flustered. She had to focus; she was here for a reason. A very important reason.

It was just that . . . well, the very first time she ever saw *Scarface* was at Hobson's house, freshman year. A bunch of them (Noah, Sunday, Allison, Boyce Sutton, and her) had all gone over to the Crowes' place in New Canaan during a long week-end, when Mr. and Mrs. Crowe were out of town. Hobson's older brother, Walker, had been there, too—supposedly to keep an eye on things. But Walker had just locked himself away in his room the whole time with a bunch of *his* friends, cranking music and smoking pot from a four-foot bong.

Anyway, while Hobson and Mackenzie and the rest of their crew were watching the movie, Hobson had asked Mackenzie to come down to the basement to help him bring up a case of soda. It was dark down there. Pitch black. Hobson said he couldn't find the light switch. They kept stumbling and giggling. Mackenzie held his hand so she wouldn't get lost. They'd ended up making out for about five minutes. Mackenzie had never told anyone about that—not even Sunday, and *definitely* not Allison . . . nobody. There was nothing wrong with it, of course; it had happened long before Hobson and Allison started going out. Still, for some reason, it just ended up being their little secret. Their private little moment. Something special that nobody else shared. She and Hobson had never talked about it again, either. That was the magic of it.

"So do you wanna knock boots or not?" Hobson asked.

Her jaw dropped. *Now* she understood. "No!" she cried. "You think I came over here to *fool around* with you?"

He shrugged innocently.

"Hobson . . . it's a—it's a *Thursday night,* for one thing," she stammered. "Check-in is in less than an hour—"

"I'll be quick, baby."

She rolled her eyes. "Hobson, I came here to get you and Allison back together." She sighed and sat down at the foot of his bed. "See this book?" She

waved *Past Life Regression Therapy* in front of his face.
"I'm gonna use it to hypnotize you—"

"Oooh, I like the sound of that," he interrupted. "*Hyp-no-tize.*" He enunciated the word with
a peculiar lisp. "Sounds freaky."

Mackenzie shook her head. "No, no, this is serious," she insisted. "I'm going to search your past
lives to find the reason you broke up with Allison.
It'll be really cool." She shifted on the bed to face
him. He was starting to look dubious. "Everybody
was somebody famous at least once in their past
lives. I was Janis Joplin. And I bet that you—"

"Yo, why're you always talking about Janis Joplin?
That honey is *nasty,* yo! You ever seen any pictures of her?
I mean, she's, like, the reason they invented Oxy Ten."

Mackenzie frowned. "Janis is not *nasty,*" she muttered. "Anyway, that's not the point—"

"Mack, can I ask you sum'm?"

She exhaled. Her shoulders drooped. "You
won't let me finish?"

"Just answer me this," he said. "Now, I know
you're way into astrology. And I'm a bit of a stargazer
myself. And, see, I'm a Taurus, right? Born on May
fourth." His tone seemed to shift a little. There was
less Mack-A-Lot, more old-school Hobson. "And
Allison is a Leo. Now I know that *you* know that bulls
and lions butt heads."

Mackenzie nodded. She couldn't argue with that one.

"And I *love* Allison, you know? Just not in that way. She and I just aren't meant to be together. I've known that for a long time. And I hope someday we can look back and laugh at all this. But a Taurus and a Scorpio . . . that's a match made in heaven." He pointed toward the ceiling. "Literally, yo. Can you dig that?"

"Yeah, but . . ." Mackenzie couldn't finish. She didn't even know what she wanted to say. Hobson was right. She'd pointed out that very fact herself on many occasions. Scorpios and Tauruses *were* good together. Miss Burke was a Taurus, after all.

But . . . what did that *mean*?

Okay, maybe Hobson and Allison really weren't meant for each other. (Even though both of their names ended in "son.") Maybe they would just have to come to terms with this breakup. But it certainly didn't mean that Hobson and *Mackenzie* should become an item.

She shook her head.

This was all happening so fast; it was too weird, too unexpected. Never in a million years would she have dreamt that Hobson would make a move on her. Not tonight. Although her horoscope *did* say to look for romance in unexpected places . . . and yes, she liked Hobson and thought he was cute (who didn't think he was cute?), but there was no way she'd hurt Allison like that. . . .

"What are you thinking?" Hobson murmured, scooting closer to her.

Mackenzie bit her lip. She stared down at her lap. Her heart started racing. "It's a Thursday night," she said.

Hobson laughed gently. "All right," he said. "Well, at least hang out for a bit. Lemme check out this past life business." He took the book from her hands. "You know, I could see myself getting into this, too." He flipped through the first couple of pages. "Hypnotism and what-not. Does this teach you how to get in touch with dead people?"

"I . . . uh, don't know." She turned to him.

He was hunched over the book, a very serious expression on his face.

Man, Mackenzie thought. Sunday and Allison hadn't even *looked* at the book. From what she could tell, Hobson was more open-minded than her two best friends. *My two best friends.* But, in a way, she'd always known that.

"Cool!" he whispered, his blue eyes wide. "It says in the intro that a person can have up to seventy lives." He paused for a second, then tossed the book aside. "Oh, that reminds me. I picked up this album I want you to hear." He hopped up from the bed and walked over to the stereo, then ejected the CD that was playing. "These guys believe in reincarnation, too. Ever hear of Earth, Wind & Fire?"

She hesitated, trying to think. "I'm not sure."

He put the CD in its case, then grabbed another one from the massive collection next to the turntables. "I saw that these guys were sampled by Brand Nubian," he said, popping the disc into the player. He turned the volume up a little. "So I just had to pick it up. Dig it, yo."

There was a funky little guitar riff, then the bass kicked in—then all of a sudden, the walls were shaking with drums and horns and a wild voice singing: *"Ye-ahh!"*

Her heart fluttered again. Wow. The music was like nothing she'd ever heard; it was so bottom-heavy, so dense.

"When you wish upon a star," the voice sang. *"Your dreams will take you very far. . . ."*

Hobson grinned, nodding his head in time. Mackenzie couldn't help but do the same thing. Where did he find this stuff? It was probably really rare—the kind of album you could only buy at one of those teeny, hole-in-the-wall record shops in New York City. She couldn't believe he'd made the effort to search to the genuine source of Brand Nubian's music, the inspiration. Not only was he open-minded, he was also so . . . *deep.*

But then, she'd always known that, too.

He sat back next to her. "You like this?" he murmured.

She nodded. "Yeah."

Oh, jeez—why not? She grabbed him and mashed her lips against his. Fate was fate, after all. You could only argue with the stars for so long.

Notes exchanged between Noah and Winslow Ellis in Miss Burke's class, Friday

So, NOAH. WHAT DID MISS BURKE WANT TO TALK TO YOU ABOUT?

Nothing. She wanted to know if I'd finished reading 1984.

LIAR. COME ON, BIG MAN. WHAT DID YOU GUYS TALK ABOUT?

1984. You know, we should stop passing notes like this. We're cheating ourselves out of an education.

DUDE, YOU'RE PLAYING THIS ALL WRONG. IF I WAS YOU, I'D GET THE CAMPUS TALKING. YOU AND MISS BURKE. YOU KNOW WHAT I'M SAYING. I'LL BACK YOU UP.

You're too kind. I'll let you know if I need your services. Good-bye, Winnie.

16

Click-click. Click.

Fred held his breath, squinting at his doorknob in the darkness.

Click.

All right. He wasn't imagining things. Somebody was trying to open the door. Somebody was trying to get into his room. At two o'clock in the freaking morning. He tossed his sheets aside and bolted out of bed. He knew damn well who it was, too. Burwell. The guy was sneaking into his room at night while Fred was asleep, spying on him. Good thing Fred had started locking up. The nerve of that fat jerk. But Fred was going to put an end to this. Right now. He dashed forward and turned the lock, throwing the door open.

"What the hell do you—"

He gasped. It wasn't Burwell. It was *Sunday*.

Fred shook his head, swallowing. He was suddenly very conscious of the fact that he was wearing only boxers. But something was majorly wrong here. In a flash, he could see that Sunday was a wreck: She wasn't wearing normal clothes, either—just pajamas and an overcoat. And sneakers. Sunday Winthrop never wore sneakers. Her hair hung in front of her face. Her eyes were red. She had a bag slung over her shoulder, stuffed full. *Holy*— Maybe she was planning on running away from school.

"Can I come in?" she breathed. Her voice was hoarse.

He nodded, too stunned to speak. He stepped aside and closed the door behind them.

There was a bump, followed by a short screech of metal.

"Ow!" she hissed. "What's this—"

"You gotta watch out for the folding chair," he whispered. She was groping in the darkness. He took her arm and carefully guided her around the chair to the bed. "What's wrong? What's going on?"

"I . . . it's a long story." She sighed and slumped down beside him. Her bag slipped off her shoulder with a thud. The mattress squealed. "I just can't stay in my room anymore."

He blinked, staring at her shadowy form. "Why not? What happened?"

She laughed miserably. "Well, for one thing, Allison wouldn't let me decorate it. She forced me to let a famous Swedish designer decorate it. Sven Larsen. Ever heard of him?"

"I . . . uh . . ." He shook his head.

"It doesn't matter. I tried to be a good friend to her. I really did." Her voice grew strained. "I mean things have always been tense between us. . . ."

Oh, no. Was she going to cry? Fred wasn't good in these kinds of situations. He didn't even know what kind of a situation this *was.* He'd just been asleep, for God's sake. He reached over to put a hand on her shoulder—then stopped himself at the last second. Maybe he shouldn't try to touch her right now. She wasn't herself. She was obviously teetering on the edge of some kind of deep, heavy, black abyss. He should just listen.

"Last night, Mackenzie and I found her going through my garbage," Sunday continued. She took a deep breath. Her voice finally stopped shaking. "And I realized I just couldn't take it anymore. I mean, I had to go back and sleep there last night, and it killed me. Allison and I aren't talking. We haven't exchanged one word in twenty-four hours. And even Mackenzie is starting to weird out on me. Last night, she was all like, 'We have to get Allison and Hobson back together. Then everything will be cool.' And today, she was like, 'There's no way they're getting back together. None at all.' And she wouldn't tell me why she'd changed her mind."

Fred nodded blankly. He had no idea what she was talking about. But he couldn't tell if that was because he was so groggy, or because she was so incoherent. Maybe both.

"Uh . . . why was Allison going through your garbage?" he asked.

"To find this." She reached into her coat pocket and pulled out a crumpled piece of paper. "A letter I wrote you."

Fred stared at the dark silhouette of her face. "A letter . . ." He left the words hanging.

She laughed softly and looked down at her lap. "Yeah, it's funny," she said. "Because in a way, I should actually *thank* Allison for what she did. If I hadn't caught her, I wouldn't have changed my mind." She turned and handed him the paper. "You see, I threw this out. I wasn't going to give it to you. But after the fight with Allison, I realized I *had* to give it to you. I should have followed my first instincts all along."

"You, ah, want me to read it right now?" he asked. His throat was dry. It was a good thing she couldn't see his fingers. They were trembling.

She lifted her shoulders in a noncommittal shrug. "If you want."

What the hell is my problem? Of course she wanted him to read it right now. Why else would she have snuck over here at two in the morning? Fred leaned over and turned on the bed lamp. He squinted and blinked for a few seconds as his eyes adjusted to the glare, then held the paper up to his face. The top part was smudged. His eyes flashed down the page.

just think it's so cool what you tried to do for Tony. And it's strange, because when I was walking into the dining hall that morning, I was feeling so sorry for myself—thinking about how powerless I was, about how everybody else always seems to make my decisions FOR me. But when I saw what you did for Tony, I realized that I'm the only one to blame for that. I mean, the reason I feel trapped is because I've always been scared of taking risks, to stand up and do what's right.

His breath started coming fast.

It was a confessional . . . although not a fully articulated one. It was vague. He soaked up the words. And the more he read, the more he realized that it was *deliberately* vague. Yes. It danced around the real issue—in a beautiful, subtle way. It hinted at the true feeling behind what was actually written.

Like a poem. Or a really good Bob Dylan song. As he continued, a quote from *Psychotic Reactions and Carburetor Dung* sprang into his mind. It fit Sunday perfectly. She wore *"a facade as brittle as it was icy, which I guess means that it was bound to crack or thaw, and whatever real artistic potency lay beneath would have to stand or evaporate."*

Lester Bangs had been talking about David Bowie at the time. But it didn't matter. Because Sunday clearly had real artistic potency, too. And *hers* didn't evaporate, either. It stood. Her AB facade was too thin to mask her true identity for very long. She couldn't keep the beauty hidden. It was bound to break free sooner or later. . . .

His throat tightened. Thinking about Lester Bangs reminded him of Diane, of course. He couldn't help it. The ghost of Diane still followed him wherever he went. And he knew that deep down, no matter how much he pretended to hate her or blame her for all his misery . . . well, a part of him secretly hoped that she was still thinking about him.

But the reality was that she wasn't. (Or the chances were that she wasn't, anyway.) He had to accept that. Besides, Diane might have changed a lot. Maybe she didn't read Lester Bangs anymore. Maybe she didn't read at all. Maybe she'd turned into a female version of Hobson Crowe. Anything was possible. He had to move on. And this letter was a perfect vehicle for him to do so. Because it was *real*. It was the here-and-now. Not some fuzzy memory of a first romance that somehow grew more idyllic the further he drifted away from it. . . .

He finished reading and glanced up at her.

"So?" she murmured. "Do you?"

"Do I what?" he asked thickly.

"Do you want to get to know me better?"

His eyes fell to the page. He opened his mouth, then closed it. And until he actually answered, he wasn't sure what he was going to say.

"I do," he murmured. "But . . ."

"But?" she echoed.

He turned to her again. "Sunday, I gotta be honest with you. This letter is the most incredible thing that anyone has ever given to me. And I mean that. It took real balls. Excuse me. Courage." He cleared his throat. "It's just that . . . see, this girl broke up with me a while ago. Diane. And I still think of her all the time, and I hate myself for it—"

"Fred," Sunday whispered. She put her hand on his arm and smiled. "It's okay."

"But I'm over Diane," he insisted. "I mean, I know I should be. So I—"

"It's okay," Sunday repeated. Her smile softened.

"But I'm just, like, totally blown away by this." He shook his head at the letter. "It's the coolest thing anybody's ever said about me. I don't even know if it's true. I'm just worried I'm gonna disappoint you—"

"No, you won't," she interrupted. "It's not just the thing with Tony Viverito. It's everything. The trust fall. Spiking the punch. You're like this one-man subversive unit. You show everybody here how silly we all are. But in this excellent way. I mean, it's amazing."

Wow. Fred couldn't even respond. The way she talked about him made it seem as if he had some sort of grand plan, some kind of *vision*. But he didn't. He just acted on stupid thoughts that popped into his head. And from what he could tell, that was pretty much the only facet of his personality that separated him from everyone else at this school. A total lack of judgment.

"So I'm just gonna lay it right out on the table, all right?" she said. "Can I crash here? Tonight, I mean?"

"What, are you *kidding*?" he mumbled. "Of course. Jesus. I thought you came to tell me that you were running away. You can crash here every night of the week. As long as you want."

She laughed. "I might just have to take you up on that."

Fred tried to smile. His face reddened. He suddenly wished he hadn't turned on the light. He edged away from her, rubbing his palms on his thighs. "Well . . . okay. Whatever." He shook his head and leaned back on the bed, placing the letter on his nightstand. Then he drew in his breath. He needed to get a grip on himself. Still, if *she* were going to confess, then he supposed he should, too. "You know, it's funny. I mean, I'm totally psyched you're here, right now. But, uh . . . see, I always planned on borrowing a bunch of obscure hip-hop CDs from Hobson before I invited you up here for the first time. That and the—"

"CDs of the songs that were originally sampled," she finished dryly. She patted his shoulder. "Yeah. The Noah Percy method of chick-scamming. Save your money. I know all about it."

He laughed. She really *was* artful. With that one little offhand joke, his anxiety began to melt away. "Glad you cleared that up for me," he said. "Otherwise I would have made a fool out of myself."

She slipped out of her coat and tossed it over the chair. "So. I guess this is a way for you to make up for getting me in trouble that day, huh?"

"Jeez, Sunday, I don't know," he kidded. "Letting you crash here is a pretty big deal. *You* might have to do *me* a favor now."

"Like what?" She pulled off her sneakers and dropped them onto the floor.

"Like giving me my chair back so I can throw out this folding piece of crap."

Sunday grinned, giving the chair a quick once-over.

"Why? It has a certain charm. Besides, I *can't* give you the chair back. Sven Larsen threw it out. He replaced it with one of his own. One of those backless chairs that's supposed to be good for posture. My dad'll kill me if he ever finds out." She paused. "But you're right. I *should* do you a favor."

Fred swallowed. Her tone was undeniably . . . well, suggestive. But then, she'd also used the same tone of voice when she'd told him to "make a move" that day at the Marriott. Of course, he hadn't been sitting with her on a bed half-naked at two in the morning. . . .

"I think I should join your subversive unit," she continued. She sat up straight, waving her hands with a dreamy sparkle in her eyes. "I think I should join you in future trust falls and punch-spikings and whatever else you cook up. I want to help you take the BS out of boarding school. After all, Olsen said I should get involved in extracurricular activities. And I can't think of a better one than that."

Fred chuckled softly. At this point, he didn't even know what he was feeling anymore—other than completely wiped out. But somehow strangely content, too. "Hmm," he murmured. "That's a major decision. I think you better let me sleep on it."

"Agreed," she said.

Without another word, he reached over and flipped off the light, then slipped under the covers in the darkness. He mushed himself against the wall to make as much room as possible for her. She slid in beside him. Her feet brushed against his leg, causing his heart to pound momentarily. Her skin was very cold and smooth. After a few awkward bumps and a couple of wriggling maneuvers, they were both in position, side-by-side on their backs. He held his breath, waiting to see if she would touch him again, or kiss him . . . but no. Nothing happened.

And much to his surprise, he could feel a smile forming on his face.

It's better this way, he thought. *It's better to ease into it. Like the letter said. To get to know each other. That's what I should have done with Diane. If I'd gotten to know her before we hooked up, I probably wouldn't have fallen so hard. . . .*

Slowly, his pulse settled into an even rhythm. Pretty amazing. If he and Sunday remained perfectly rigid, they could fall asleep without even touching each other.

"Good night, Sunday," he said.

"Good night, Fred."

He felt her fingers on his wrist.

"Thank you," she whispered. She gave him a quick squeeze and let go.

"Any time," he said.

The Manifesto of SAFU (pronounced sah-FU): Sunday and Fred United

We, the undersigned, do solemnly swear:

1) Never to use any abbreviations (SAFU excepted) when talking to each other.

2) To devote ourselves fully to making people at Wessex see the absurdity of their own lives (ours included).

3) To unite the student body against hypocrisy and cliquedom.

4) To find out, once and for all, why an oaf like Paul Burwell can be allowed to keep a job as a math teacher at Wessex for twenty years.

5) To find out why Paul Burwell (or whoever else it could have been) planted chewing tobacco on Tony Viverito.

6) To get Kate Ramsey put on the student council.

7) To get Allison back (in a very fitting way, as yet to be determined) for making the first few weeks of Sunday's senior year hell.

8) To sabotage any and all Alumni Brat events.

9) To kill Sven Larsen.

10) Okay, maybe not #9. **But everything else.**

Sunday Winthrop

Frederick Wright

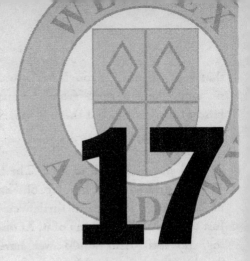

17

"You sure it's open?" Fred whispered.

"Positive," Sunday whispered back. "He never locks up."

Slowly, cautiously, they tiptoed through the darkness of Olsen's backyard—closer and closer to the door that led to the kitchen. Sunday shivered in the cold night air. Her ankles ached from hopping the back fence. But she couldn't stop smiling. This was perfect. No, it was *sublime*.

Two days ago, she wouldn't have believed that such a change was possible—that her emotions could flip-flop so completely. A hundred and eighty degrees. Instead of feeling trapped, she felt liberated. Instead of helpless, empowered. But the phrase that best summed it up . . . actually, the one that kept running through her mind (and she had no clue where it came from, because it was really kind of disgusting, but there it was): She was full of piss and vinegar.

Not literally, of course. But she felt damn good.

And she owed it all to Fred. The boy at her side. The boy dressed like a burglar. She had even dressed like a burglar, too: jeans, turtleneck, and wool cap. Just to heighten the drama of it. At one in the morning, no less. Who would ever have thought that Sunday Winthrop would sneak out two nights in a row? The old Sunday had never snuck out of her dorm at all. Not once. Sure, she'd disappeared to places unknown for a couple of long weekends. But that was after she'd already gotten permission to be off campus, anyway. She could be *suspended* for this.

Fred paused and glanced up at the darkened windows. "There's no way he'd be up, right?" His voice was barely audible over the buzzing of the crickets.

"No way," she breathed. "He lives like Ben Franklin. 'Early to bed, early to rise'—you know, the whole bit."

Fred nodded. He took a step closer.

Sunday rubbed her eyes, following behind him. She was more than a little tired. Unfortunately, the only potential snag in the whole operation was sleep deprivation. But she could live with that. Because the best part of their new pact—the real *genius* of it—was that she and Fred were keeping their relationship a secret.

Nobody would know about the Manifesto of SAFU. Nobody. Today, Sunday had even apologized to Allison. She'd sworn off Fred Wright, with Allison and Mackenzie as her witnesses. She'd gone so far as to call her parents.

Mom:	You know we have nothing personal against this Fred person.
Sunday:	I know.
Dad:	We hear he's a heck of a basketball player.
Sunday:	I know.
Mom:	It's like Headmaster Olsen said. You can't afford to be distracted right now.
Sunday:	I know.
Dad:	He's a point guard, right?
Mom:	Stop it, dear!
Dad:	Sorry.

And that was where matters stood.

Maybe someday Sunday would tell Mackenzie that she planned on sneaking out every night to sleep in Fred's room until graduation. But for now, it was better that Mackenzie didn't know. Mackenzie still thought that Sunday and Allison could salvage their friendship. She still clung to that hope. It would crush her if she knew the truth: that as long as Allison disapproved of Fred (and she always would), she and Sunday could never be friends. And all Mackenzie ever wanted was for people to get along. That was what made her happy. Sunday would never deprive Mackenzie of happiness. Mackenzie *deserved* happiness.

It was funny, though: The irony of the whole scenario was that Sunday's relationship with Fred was still totally innocent. Yes, they'd slept in the same bed. But they hadn't even *kissed.* And maybe they never would. In a way, though, that didn't even matter. Because in the eyes of Wessex, they already had. Sunday's reputation as a prude had been officially retired. Which made tonight's foray (or "forage," as Burwell would say) that much sweeter. . . .

Fred paused at the door.

"Here it goes," he murmured.

Sunday held her breath. He turned the latch.

It opened.

Fred glanced over his shoulder, grinning in the moonlight. Sunday gave him a thumbs-up. She followed him into the shadowy kitchen. She could barely see a thing except for the silhouettes of hanging pots and pans. Her pulse raced. She wanted to laugh, to dance, to shriek for joy. Especially since they were skipping straight ahead to item number seven on the Manifesto. Yes . . . they'd both agreed that it was best to take care of Allison first. While revenge was still fresh in Sunday's mind.

The plan was beautiful. Tonight, they were going to grab a bunch of Olsen's personal stationery from the rolltop desk in his living room. Then they would compose love letters to Allison. Filled with intimate details. Typed on one of those old-fashioned typewriters that Olsen had. (They'd figure out how to get that later.) Allison was just humorless enough to believe that Olsen had a crush on her. And Olsen was just enough of an odd bird to arouse her suspicion, what with his seasonal slacks and Shakespeare and bow ties. . . .

And if Allison ever *did* confront him about his advances, there would be a lovely, twisted, bizarre couple of days of confusion before they determined it was a prank. But there would be nothing to link Sunday and Fred to it. No evidence. Not even fingerprints. They were both wearing gloves. Sure, Sunday felt a little bad about playing such a cruel joke on Olsen. But not *that* bad. In a way, he'd been just as complicit as Allison in making Sunday's life hell. . . .

Fred froze at the door to the living room.

Sunday nearly slammed into him. *What the—* She gulped. Was something wrong? Fred straightened and held up a finger, frowning in the darkness. Did he hear a noise? Sunday stopped breathing. But all she heard was her own heartbeat. Fred lowered his hand and shook his head. He hurried to the rolltop desk.

"How much stationery should I take?" he hissed.

"Just a little," Sunday breathed. Her throat was dry. "Otherwise he might notice."

Fred nodded, opening the cover. He fumbled through the pens and envelopes for a few sheets of paper. Sunday's eyes darted to the archway that led to the front hall. What if Olsen woke up? What if he decided to get a drink of water? Or a late-night snack? Some milk and cookies? Maybe all that Ben Franklin stuff was a lie and he was a closet insomniac. . . .

"Got it," Fred whispered. He carefully folded the papers and tucked them into his jacket pocket, then closed the desk.

As quickly and quietly as she could, Sunday led the way back through the kitchen. She couldn't even breathe again until they were outside, until Fred had shut the back door behind them. Beads of sweat were forming on her brow. But she managed a shaky smile.

Fred, of course, seemed perfectly relaxed. He grinned at her, his eyes sparkling in the moonlight.

"Hey, can we go around front?" Sunday asked, glancing across the lawn. "I don't feel like jumping the fence again."

Fred nodded. He gently took her arm. Together they hurried around the side of the house, down a little paved path of stone.

Finally, Sunday started to calm down a little. And then she realized something. That was the closest she'd ever come to a major thrill. Pretty much. Well, there was the time last summer when she'd taken Dad's Mercedes out for a secret spin around the driveway. Pathetic. She and Fred picked up their pace when they reached the open expanse of Olsen's lawn. . . .

"Hey, look."

Fred jerked to a halt. He thrust a finger at a window on the first floor.

A bluish light was flickering behind it.

Holy—

Sunday's legs nearly gave out from under her. That was the den. Olsen must be watching TV in there. He *was* awake. And they had been less than twenty feet . . . Okay, time to get the hell out of here. She couldn't fake it anymore; this was *way* too risky for her comfort level. But Fred let go of her arm. He crouched down in the darkness and ducked toward the window.

Sunday glared at him. What the hell was he doing? Maybe the adrenaline was clouding his judgment. But she couldn't stop him; she couldn't speak.

He scurried closer and closer, then peeked inside.

Sunday was practically hyperventilating now. Was this really necessary?

He waved her over.

She shook her head. She doubted she could move, anyway; her ankles felt as if they were made of Jell-O. But he waved again, more emphatically.

This is so stupid. . . .

Clenching her jaw, she crept up to his side.

He pointed through the pane of glass.

Then she froze.

Olsen was sitting on his couch, sipping a cocktail of some kind. He wasn't alone.

Sitting to his right was Winslow Ellis.

At one o'clock in the morning.

The lights were off. They were both staring at the TV. Their faces were grotesque in the uncertain, shifting glow. And on the screen . . .

Sunday's eyes narrowed.

Oh, my God. She clamped a hand over her mouth.

For a terrible second, she was worried she might yak all over Olsen's lawn. Well, either that or burst into laughter. Or scream.

They were watching a porn movie.

No doubt about it. There were two bodies on the screen, male and female, squirming on a couch. Buck-ass naked. The film looked homemade, too . . .

at least judging from the low camera angle and the fuzzy quality of the videotape. The male seemed pretty young. . . .

Noah?

That was . . . Noah. On-screen. Sunday would be able to spot that brown cowlick anywhere.

She blinked—once, twice, very rapidly. Maybe she was more tired than she thought. In fact, maybe she wasn't even awake. Maybe she was back in her suite, or in Fred's room, caught in the throes of some very vivid and utterly absurd dream. . . .

"Let's go," Fred breathed.

Sunday nodded. Yes, it was time to split. Mission over . . . Fred was already backing away from the window. Without a word, they broke into a full-fledged sprint.

Get away from the house. Get away . . .

Strangely, Sunday had only one thought. And it wasn't that she'd just seen Noah Percy's naked body on a TV screen. No, it was that Mackenzie was right, after all. Mackenzie Wilde was actually *right*. Winnie and Olsen *were* involved in something nefarious. Something beyond nefarious. Something so sick that she couldn't even possibly begin to make sense out of it . . .

Before she knew it, she and Fred were dashing up the front steps of Ellis Hall. How had they gotten here so quickly? Under normal circumstances, it took a good five minutes to walk from Olsen's mansion to Fred's dorm. Sunday shook her head as they tiptoed up the spiral staircase. Clearly, her brain was short-circuiting from information overload. She needed to sit. Once they were safely inside Fred's room, they could sit down and collect themselves. They could try to figure this all out. . . .

Fred opened the door and flicked on the light.

"Jesus!" he shouted, flinching.

The color drained from Sunday's face.

They weren't alone.

Mr. Burwell was sitting in the metal chair.

He looked very content. Not tired at all. His hands were folded in his lap. He smiled up at them. Tonight's double-breasted suit was olive green.

"Well, well, well," he said. "Little late to be taking a forage outside, isn't it?"